# UNDER HER ROOF

## ACCIDENTALLY UNDERCOVER

ALLISON TEMPLE

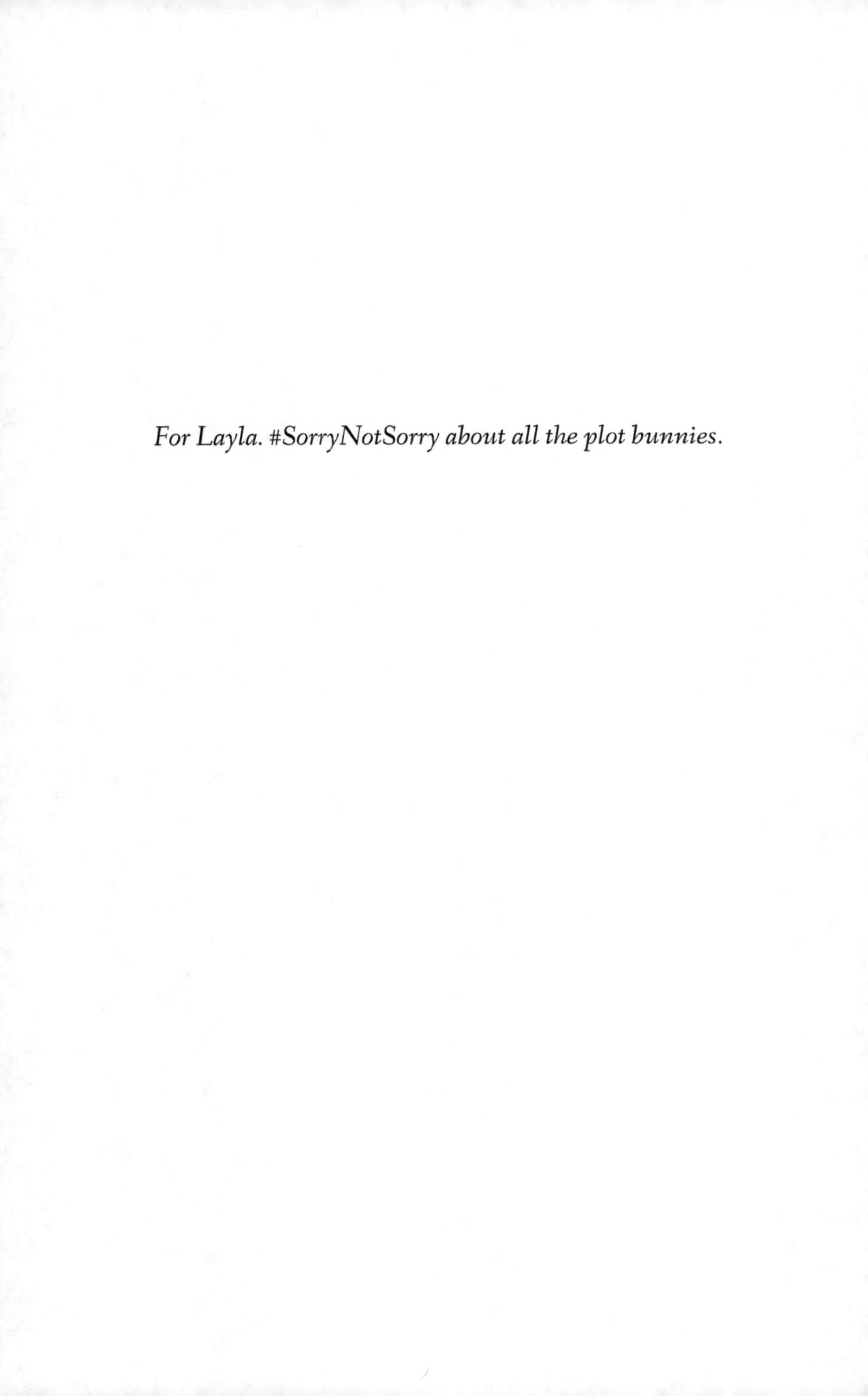

*For Layla. #SorryNotSorry about all the plot bunnies.*

# ONE

IT'S a dark and stormy night as six strangers wait for a boat that will take them to a remote private island.

Okay, that's not quite true. It's a grey and dreary afternoon. It rained for a while around lunchtime, and the clouds overhead say it's going to rain again. Truthfully, the forecast for the final weekend of summer in the Muskokas is not promising.

Also, I'm the only stranger here. We're standing on the dock at the marina, and while I know no one, the other five people here are chatting among themselves. There's an elegant man and woman. They're both white, but the man's black suit and slicked-back ponytail look out of place here in cottage country. The silver in his beard says he's old enough to not give a fuck what people think, though. The woman is in a pink chiffon dress and flat gold sandals. Everything about her is graceful, from the arch of her neck to the way she leans in to speak softly into his ear.

The other three people are two men and a woman. One man is older. Shorter. Still white. He's in a tweed jacket and pressed blue shirt, and even though the air has lost its summertime humidity, he keeps mopping his bald head with a handkerchief. The other man and the woman, both in their early thirties, are talking loudly and excitedly to each other. His dark hair and tanned skin speak to some Mediterranean heritage. Her black hair and dark eyes are distinctively Asian, but her accent is one hundred percent Toronto. The older man keeps trying to join them, speaking in a posh French accent—as in French from France, not the throaty growl of Montreal French —and while the woman is happy enough to engage, the younger man positions his body so that he's constantly cutting the bald man out of the conversation.

"Do you really think they have a Chateau Saint-Michel? I heard it's a 1987. Of course, an '88 would be bigger but also out of our price range, right?" The young man laughs at the woman. The sound is too loud, echoing out over the water. The woman smiles, but she also slides her hand in his, and her silent squeeze warns him he's being too much. But he keeps laughing, and the bald man keeps mopping at his head and looking uncomfortable.

The point is, though, they all have someone to chat with, and I'm left standing here like a lump. I glance back to where my car is parked in the marina lot. Still time to leave. But leaving admits defeat. It means Sloan wins, and I can't let that happen. So I pull the neck of my yellow rain jacket tighter as the air threatens precipitation again and wait.

Finally, Murray emerges from the cabin of the boat tied up at the dock. He's got grease on his shirt and the sweat stain on his ball cap starts at the brim and goes halfway up the frayed Murray's Marina logo on his brow. He winces as he turns the key, but his smile is all relieved sunshine as the engine roars to life. The people around me take an apprehensive step back, but Murray waves them forward.

"Okay, folks! Let's get moving before she decides to pack it in for the season after all."

Nervous glances are exchanged while the outboard chugs in the water, but one by one, the strangers board the vessel. It's the only way to get to Ross Island, after all, which is the reason everyone has come.

Though my reason is a little different than the others'.

"I haven't seen you at one of these before," the young woman says once we're underway. The boat is Murray's old twenty-eight-footer, and there's only enough seating for the six of us, so I'm stuck sitting squeezed between her and the elegant woman in the pink dress.

"One of these?" I ask.

"The auction." Her smile is wide and open. Her hair is pulled back in a high ponytail that sways with the bouncing motion of the boat. "It's so convenient that it's close to home, isn't it?"

Closer than she knows. I give her a tight grin that she can take as agreement or not. Mostly I want it to be a dismissal. These people are leeches. Parasites. Whether they realize it or not, they're here to feed on what's left of my family.

Though I wouldn't mind feeding Sloan to the fishes. She's refused to answer my calls for the last two weeks, but she can't avoid me if we're standing face-to-face. If that doesn't work, I'll throw her to the sharks . . . the legal kind, at least. But I'd rather not sue her. She is my sister, after all.

"I'm Laurel," the woman says, clearly still intent on learning my life story. She holds out her hand to shake, and I have to twist my body to take it without elbowing the elegant woman in the process. She at least seems happy to pretend I don't exist.

"Gillian."

"This is my boyfriend, Chris," Laurel says.

"Maybe you've heard of us?" he says with a confident grin. When I shake my head, he laughs. "Wine babe? No?"

I still have no idea. "I'm really sorry."

He laughs again, loud even over the sound of the boat, and slings an arm over Laurel's shoulder. "Wine babe! It's our Instagram account."

"Oh. That's . . ." Thankfully, before I can embarrass myself further, the boat rises up and comes down hard on a wave, making us all bounce. Murray curses. Laurel shrieks. The bald man looks green. The elegant couple don't look like anything odd has happened. They're whispering between themselves in the hard, percussive sounds of a language I don't recognize. Russian, maybe? Something Eastern European, at least. My ability to speak foreign languages crashed and burned in high school after French class stopped being mandatory. I can ask where the washroom is, but the only other sentence I remember is *Placez le pamplemousse dans la poubelle,* and so far, the opportunity to tell someone to put the grapefruit in the garbage can has never presented itself.

The clouds swell, and the sky darkens.

"Looks like it might rain again," Murray says. "We've still got a bit before we get to the island. There are drinks in the cabin. You can help yourself."

The promise of libations is enough to send everyone else below. I stay where I am. Hopefully, they're not too disappointed to find Murray has stocked the cooler with his favourite brand of light beer and not a 1987 Chemain Saint-Domaine or whatever Laurel was talking about. Wine has never been my thing.

"How are you doing, Gilly?" Murray's question draws me away from thoughts I don't want to visit. I give him the same smile I give everyone who asks that question because the answer is very long and most people don't actually want to hear it.

"I'm okay," I say. Murray's been running the marina for as long as I can remember. I wouldn't say he was exactly friends with my dad, but you can't buy gas, beer, and potato chips from the same person for over fifty years and not at least be friendly.

"Been busy at the house," he says. "I've been driving people back and forth for the last month. A lot of guys in suits." He gives me a wink, but the words make my face go hot with anger, even in the wind. Guys in suits have no business up here, especially not at Dad's house. But apparently, Sloan disagrees. Hence the need for this urgent conversation.

The rain clouds continue to loom, and the wind comes up, making the boat roll harder in the growing chop. The guests stay below, and maybe Murray did break out a few bottles of vino for the occasion because every so often the clink of glasses filters toward me.

The house, as Murray called it, sits atop the chunk of rock known as Ross Island. There had been a Mr. Ross, maybe a hundred years ago. He owned a string of newspapers in Ontario and Quebec and built a modest cottage for his family on the island. Over time, the modest cottage was expanded and rebuilt until now it's hardly a cottage anymore. When my parents got divorced, Dad kept the house up here and Mom took the one in Toronto. Sloan and I spent most of the school year in the city, but as soon as class was out, we were here. Late sunsets and lazy days. That's what I remember.

But not anymore. Not if Sloan gets her way.

"Oh, it's bigger than I thought it would be." Laurel has come to stand beside me. We're getting our first glimpse of the top of the roof peeking out from between the tall spruce and pine trees that cover the island. Laurel sounds a little breathless, and her cheeks are pink. She turns her glassy gaze on me, and I give her another wordless smile. It has to be bad etiquette to show up at an exclusive wine auction already tipsy, but what do I know? "I heard he lived here year-round. Can you imagine how lonely it would be in the winter? How would he even get things like groceries?"

"Snowmobile," I say without thinking. "Or a ski plane if the ice is thick enough." Dad sold the plane a few years ago. A lifetime of being hunched over his typewriter meant his eyesight wasn't what it used to be, and he finally agreed flying a plane in a snowstorm with 20/100 vision wasn't the best idea.

"Did you read about that somewhere?" Laurel asks. "I looked up his Wikipedia page before we left, but I don't remember it saying anything about that. Arnold Fletcher." She shudders. "They made me read *Frost Burn* in high school. It was so depressing. Did you ever read it?"

Did I? I can't even say anymore. Probably it was on a syllabus somewhere sometime. But when you're the daughter of the man who wrote "the most significant piece of Canadian fiction of the last half century"—thank you *Globe & Mail* book review—you don't actually need to read the book to know the plot. Anyone who ever came to the house asked him about it. Where did Dad get his inspiration? Did he ever live in Saskatchewan? Is the character based off his wife or someone else? I know all the answers.

Laurel doesn't wait to hear them, though, before she says, "Do you think it's true?"

"What's true?" I ask, hair prickling on my nape.

She glances around like she's worried someone's listening, even though you'd have to be standing right beside her to hear over the roar of the boat engine.

"About how he died?"

My heart sinks.

"I—" But I don't even have any way to finish that sentence.

Fortunately, Laurel doesn't seem to be worried about having an actual conversation.

"I heard it was suicide," she whispers. "That they found him—"

"Heart attack," I say quickly, because the end of her sentence was going to be disgusting and untrue. "It was a heart attack."

It was too. But I'm familiar with the other stories. The rumors. The media had a field day. Or field days, I guess. About four of them, before the death of famous author Arnold Fletcher fell off the front page in favour of the government's latest collusion scandal. But in those four days, the news regurgitated every rumor they could find on Twitter. A heart attack. Suicide. A robbery gone wrong. Drugs. Alcohol. Didn't matter if it was true. All they had to do was copy and paste.

But it was a heart attack, plain and simple. And the rumors that he'd spent a week or a month or the entire winter dead on his study floor are lies too. He can't have been dead for more than twelve hours. He'd been having some work done at the house and called the contractor just after eight in the evening, then the same contractor found his body by eight the following morning. The nitro spray was in his hand. As deaths go, it's about as cut-and-dried as it gets.

Laurel's brows are pinched together like she's trying to decide if she wants to debate the details with me. If she does, I might toss her overboard. But before we can get to that, the boat rounds the final point of land, and the house comes into full view.

"Look." I point out the sprawling timber frame creation. It glows in the late afternoon sun.

"Ohh." Laurel's eyes light up. "Chris! Babe! We're here!" She hurries away, and the moment of tension she probably didn't even feel goes with her.

As we pull up to the dock, Murray goes about tying us off behind the small white sailboat that's already there. I groan softly. Bert and Didi are here. Exactly the people I least want to see . . . after Sloan.

Without the boat motor running to cover it, the sound of laughter wafts down from the elevated deck on the front of the house. People are milling around. At one point, a few heads turn toward us while Murray helps the guests step off onto solid ground.

"Hey!" someone calls. Sloan's blonde head and smiling face appear over the balcony rail. She waves like a queen acknowledging her subjects, but her voice is very much princess-on-a-joyride. "Get up here! The party's already started!"

"Can you wait?" I ask Murray as the others make their way up the winding cedar staircase. "I won't be here long."

"You're not staying?" he asks, but he glances at the sky, where the clouds are hanging lower and darker than before. "I hear it's going to be quite the weekend."

Laughter sounds again, making my throat hurt. I shake my head. "I need to talk to Sloan for a minute." Hopefully, the sight of me in front of her will make her realize what an utter selfish pain in the ass she's being, and we'll get this resolved quickly.

Distantly, thunder rumbles, and Murray grimaces.

"I can't be out in a storm," he says. "Kelsey gets scared."

I sigh. Kelsey is his ancient labrador. She panics with any kind of loud noise. Thunder. Fireworks. Once during Canada Day celebrations, she freaked out, escaped from inside Murray's boat, and jumped into the lake trying to get away.

"Please. I'll be quick," I say.

"Why don't you stay the night?" he asks. "One last visit?"

I ball my hands into fists. I'm not here for sentiment. Right now, I need anger and purpose, not soft feelings about old memories. Also, it's not like I packed anything for an overnight. No toothbrush or clean underwear.

The lights aren't on at the boathouse. However many people

Sloan's invited for this thing, they must all be staying up at the main house. There's an old guestroom in the boathouse loft, though, assuming Sloan hasn't cleared it out. I don't mind sleeping among the spiders for one night. Wouldn't want to stress Murray and poor Kelsey. I'll figure out which is the most expensive bottle of wine in Dad's cellar and drink myself to sleep. It'll have the added benefit of pissing Sloan off because it's one less bottle she can sell. Two birds. One stone. Totally worth a little tooth fuzz in the morning.

"Come get me bright and early?" I try. "Nine o'clock?"

Thunder rumbles again. Murray nods. "I'm bringing everyone else for ten. How about that?"

That's too many hours to spend here, and yet it may not be enough. I have to convince my sister not to sell this place. I square my shoulders as Murray pushes the boat back toward the lake.

I can do this.

There are eighty-nine steps from the water to the house. I counted them as a kid, and now I do it as a reflex. One, two . . . forty-four, forty-five. Sloan's voice interrupts my counting, which only makes me angrier.

"Wait until you see the cellar," she's telling someone, voice a little too loud. "It's a fire sale, basically. Everything must go."

Like the house? Dad hasn't even been dead for six months. After the funeral, my sister and I agreed we'd wait before making any big decisions. And yet somehow, Sloan's been bringing guys in suits up here to check things out, and now she's selling off the wine cellar. So it's time to talk.

As I come around the top of the steps, Sloan has her back to me. She's chatting with a middle-aged white man wearing glasses, a pressed white button-down, and loafers. He's everything inoffensive and upper-class. When he gestures toward her, a heavy watch with a gold band appears under his cuff. She laughs again, tipping her head back so her hair cascades down her back. He's too old to be a potential boyfriend, and Sloan's got a partner back in the city. Bruno. They spend half their time in Toronto and half in the Azores where Bruno has an artist's studio. The loafer man would need a ton of money to compete with Bruno's creative spirit and raw animal magnetism. That was how Sloan described him when they first met. I've never seen the appeal. All I know is Bruno spent Dad's funeral texting.

Whoever Loafers is, he'll have to step aside, because I need a word with my sister.

"Gilly!"

A hand settles on my shoulder, and before I can even respond, I get enveloped in a tight bear hug. The smell around me immediately turns to sunscreen and cigars. It's familiar. Overwhelming. Like I'm being crushed by the love child of a gorilla and a boa constrictor.

"Hi, Bert," I gasp.

"Oh, it's so good to see you. Sloan said you weren't coming." He slaps my back so hard I cough, but then he releases me so air rushes back into my lungs. I'm staring up at the face of my dad's oldest friend. Bert—Robert if he's sitting across from you at the negotiating table—smiles down at me with twinkling blue eyes. Bert and his wife, Didi, own the house across from ours. It's been in Didi's family for four generations. They met on the lake nearly sixty years ago. Bert was a sailing instructor at the yacht club. Didi was the party girl looking for a fun time in town every weekend. They're basically a two-headed monster. Bert and Didi. Everyone knows Bert and Didi. He took early retirement right as I was finishing high school, and they've been mainstays in the lake's social scene ever since.

"Hi," I say, still gasping.

"I'm so glad you made it." He drags me into another bone-crushing hug, then says over my shoulder, "Didi. Look. Look who came."

"Thanks," I say, trying to extricate myself, "But I really—" Sloan has stopped talking to Loafers and has moved on to the bald man from the boat.

"Gilly. Oh, what a nice surprise."

Too late. Didi pulls me into a fresh round of hugs. Unlike Bert, hugging Didi feels like hugging a scarecrow. The bones of her thin body poke at me in uncomfortable places. But as we part, her expression is nothing but friendly sympathy.

"How are you doing?" she asks. "I didn't expect you to be up here again."

Why wouldn't I? I thought there'd be lots of time. I glance again toward Sloan. She's eyeing the bald guy like he might have a disease.

"Oh, it's so nice to see you," Bert says, patting my back. "This weekend is so exciting. Sloan was so smart to reach out to me about the wine." He laughs, and Didi joins him. Together, they are the king and queen of mingling. Bert has perfected the art of the summer barbecue that runs for a whole weekend. And Didi is the kind of society wife who shows up in magazine photos taken at charity galas where she's standing next to old men who have titles like "Right Honourable" next to their names.

Didi pokes me as she snorts in a surprisingly unladylike way. Her skin is flawless, no doubt toned, and peeled, and everything else until it has the texture of a newborn's backside. "Come meet Vincent," she says, and before I can protest, she's pulling me to where loafer man is now having a hurried conversation with the bald man. Sloan is standing to one side, looking annoyed to no longer be the centre of attention. As we approach, she ducks away and the bald man follows quickly.

Loafer man—Vincent, I assume—adjusts his cuffs and gives us all a confident smile.

"Vincent," Didi says, holding an arm out to welcome him into our little circle. "This is our dear friend, Gilly."

"Gillian," I say, holding out a hand, because no one who met me after age fifteen calls me Gilly.

"A pleasure," he says, his voice curling around vowels that aren't easily identifiable as Canadian or American or any other particular -an.

"Vincent is our guest of honour," Bert says, puffing his chest out.

Vincent ducks his head. "Flattery will get you nowhere, Robert."

"It gets me everywhere." Bert punches at his shoulder. It's probably meant to be friendly, but Vincent rocks on his feet. He's younger than Bert but older than me. Other than that, his age could be anything between forty and sixty. His hair is jet black and his skin is tanned. Hard to say if it's sun or genetics. Regardless, he looks completely at ease here.

Bert continues speaking. "Didi and I met Vincent at an auction in Boston. A whole collection of Bordeaux."

Didi nods eagerly. "I've never seen Bertie so excited. He spent close to ninety thousand dollars before the weekend was over."

He kisses the side of her head as they preen. Beside them, Vincent looks pleased.

"You've both been very kind with your purchases and for inviting me this weekend," he says.

"Of course you were invited. You have the best palate in the business," Bert says. Vincent makes deprecating noises, but Bert keeps on blustering. "Remember that blind tasting you invited us to?"

Didi claps her hands. "Oh, that was so impressive. Gilly,

you should have seen it. He identified fifteen different wines on the first try without seeing a single label."

"Right down to the vineyard and year." Bert chuckles. "Vinnie finds the best hidden gems, don't you? Remember that '75 Clos du Forge you sold last year? They said there were none left. But you found two in that old woman's basement. I'd have bought them both, but . . ." He whistles as he wags a hand like he's been burnt. "Too hot for my wallet. One had to do."

"What can I say? It's a gift." Vincent smiles the smile of a man who knows he has a captive audience. "I even have a special surprise for this weekend. A few offerings from my own private collection that I thought would be appropriate to complement the wines in the cellar."

Bert and Didi ooh and ahh.

"What did you bring?" Didi asks.

Vincent's smile widens and reveals blindingly white teeth. "It wouldn't be a surprise if I told you, now, would it?"

They laugh like it's the funniest thing they've ever heard. The conversation continues on to something about vintages and terroirs, but Sloan is heading toward the house. Now is my chance. If I can catch her inside, we can get this resolved without an audience.

"Excuse me. I really should say hi to my sister."

They let me go without any protest, still congratulating each other on past purchases and Vincent's talent. I follow after Sloan, hurrying as she disappears through the French doors that lead to the dining room. I'm almost inside when a voice I never expected to hear in a million years says my name in quiet astonishment.

"Gillian?"

Oh, for god's sake. It's like a bad movie. Have all of my ghosts come to haunt me?

"What are you doing here?" she asks, even while I'm frozen

to the spot, watching Sloan head toward the kitchen inside. My fingernails are digging into my palms, and I don't even remember making the fists. But slowly, I turn and find myself looking into the face of the one person I never expected to see here. The person I said I never wanted to see again.

"What am *I* doing here?" I ask. "What are *you* doing here? I told you to never come here."

Standing on the deck, looking every inch the perfect polished goddess, is Amanda. Six years ago, on this very spot, she broke my heart, and I can't stop the anger that wells up in me at the sight of her now.

"Get the hell out of my house," I say.

# TWO

ONCE UPON A TIME, I met a princess. Okay, she wasn't a princess, she was a banker, but she walked through the hotel ballroom with all the regal poise of a queen. We were at some charity fundraiser thing where Didi and Bert had sponsored a table, and at the last minute, a couple of guests backed out. Dad was in the city for a book signing, so Bert begged Dad to take the seats, and in turn, Dad begged me to join him. I had zero interest in doing it, but with the short notice, there were no other options. None of Dad's publishing friends were available, and Sloan was overseas with Bruno. So I'd done my best to wrangle a dress and my hair and makeup and showed up to save the children or feed the whales or whatever cause Didi felt like sponsoring that night.

And then, Amanda walked through the room, and it didn't matter what the cause was or that my toes were going numb in a pair of stilettos I found at the back of my closet and didn't remember buying. She was in a halter-neck dress made of green silk. Watching the way it floated over her skin made me shiver. Dad noticed it and asked if I was cold.

I'm not the sort of person who approaches other people. I've always been small. Pocket-size, if we're being honest. I'm used to being quite literally overlooked. My work as a graphic designer means I spend most of my time behind a desk. But that night, as I watched Amanda settle at the table next to ours, I knew if I didn't speak to her, I'd always wonder what opportunity I'd missed. It didn't matter if our conversation turned out to be professional or if we became the kind of friends who text every couple of months, promise to get together, and never actually get together.

In the end, I'd slid into an empty chair next to hers while someone was making a speech about wallaby rescue or whatever, and not long after, she was leading me upstairs to her hotel room where I got to find out exactly how much of an opportunity this really was.

Amanda Mulgrave was born in Vancouver and moved to Ontario to do her MBA. She works for a wealth management firm on Bay Street and may not be a true queen in the end, but she is the queen of mixing with high society and making them believe she can take them even higher. In short, she's very good at her job, and the fact that she found me interesting at all was dazzling. I've always been the serious levelheaded younger sister to Sloan's flighty artistic older sister, but as Amanda's girlfriend, I felt like I could be anything.

Or at least, I did for the first year and a half. Long enough for me to give up my condo and stop seeing a lot of my friends because I was so busy being Amanda's girlfriend that being Devon's or Sarah's or Kay's friend was something I didn't have time for anymore. Until the shine started to come off. It happens. You wake up one morning and realize the person you think you're going to devote your life to is actually a figment of your imagination, and the actual person you're living with is a workaholic with no social life beyond charity galas and art auctions for pieces you'll never be able to afford yourself. They take phone calls at all hours of the day and night and cancel plans at the last minute because "the office needs me."

Not that I'm still bitter about any of that. Of course not. But back then, no matter how much I asked her for more time or tried to steer the ship of our relationship away from the shoals, nothing changed.

And then you're shouting at them on the deck at the house, effectively trapping yourself and your now ex-girlfriend on a private island because Sloan had taken the boat into town and there was no way off for hours. I sulked in the main house while Amanda packed her things in the boathouse. Not my finest moment, but I wouldn't take back what I said. We weren't right for each other.

We still aren't.

"Amanda," I say, trying to sound so much more collected than I feel. "What a coincidence."

"There's no such thing as coincidence, Gilly. Sloan said you weren't coming," Amanda says. Her hair is shorter. She always wore it long and clipped up in a gold claw. Now it's tucked behind her ears and flares out in feathery wisps at the back of her neck. Green satin has been replaced with a taupe-coloured linen top and skirt that would look like a potato sack on me but looks casually glamourous and put-together on her lean frame.

"I wasn't invited," I say, trying not to look directly at her face. Strictly speaking, that's not true. Sloan sent an email a month or so ago. It ended with something like "You're welcome to come if you want to . . ." but the ellipses made it very clear how she felt about that. Honestly, I don't care about the wine. How much can it add up to? But then I heard about her plans for the house and that was that. Fuck the ellipses. I was coming.

Did Sloan find out somehow? Has she invited Amanda as a trap she's been waiting to spring? But if that were the case, she wouldn't have gone into the house. My sister likes a show. She'd have waited until Amanda and I saw each other and the fireworks went off instead of disappearing to check on the caterers or powder her nose.

"How are you?" Amanda asks, and the question makes me want to crawl out of my skin. How am I? How does she think I am?

"Fine." I have to fight the urge not to chew on my lip, and when I glance up, she's watching me with a sympathetic cock of her head. Next, she's going to say she was sorry to hear about Dad, and I can't have that. Amanda and Dad always got along like a house on fire. He felt possessive of her because he was there the night we met. Like somehow, he'd found a treasure and was responsible for keeping it safe. But he's not here anymore, and the treasure turned out to be tin a long time ago.

I drop my gaze as I say, "Look, it's good to see you, but I have to talk to Sloan." Then, I run. Or I try to. What I actually do is stumble as I bump into a heavy wood Muskoka chair. I don't look, but I'm pretty sure I've torn a toenail. Fuck.

Thunder rumbles again, closer this time, as I enter the house. It's quiet. Empty. Well, that's not totally true. Through the door into the kitchen, four people all dressed in chef's whites are bustling around the massive gas range and spooning little globs of something white onto crackers.

A crash behind me has me spinning to find Chris with one hand on the wall as he tries to keep from tripping over a box full of wine bottles. In his other hand, he's got his phone, and the screen reflects the shocked look on his face where he was clearly trying to take a selfie a moment before.

"Be careful with that." Vincent says, pushing Chris aside. Unlike outside when he was graciously hobnobbing with Bert and Didi, inside, his voice is firm and authoritative.

"I'm so sorry," Chris says. "I was only having a look around." He bends to pull a bottle from the box, but Vincent grabs the whole thing and hefts the box up against his chest. He's glaring at Chris, but when he spots me, his veneer of smooth professionalism slips back into place. "I brought some of my own collection for dinner tonight. There are some very rare vintages. Wouldn't want them broken before we get a chance to try them."

"Those are yours?" Chris asks, gaze lighting up. He motions to Laurel, who has been trying to take a video of the cooks in action. "Babe, come see. Vincent, did you bring the Chateau Saint-Michel? You mentioned it at the tasting in White Plains last month. I've never even seen a bottle, much less tasted it."

Vincent seems mollified with their adoration and turns his attention to them, leaving me to get back to the task at hand.

"I'm looking for Sloan?" I ask one of the cooks.

"Everyone out of my kitchen!" The order comes from a Black woman at the stove. She's got her hair pulled back in a severe bun, and her glare could sear meat. It's Reena Baker. I recognize her from the profile in *Toronto Life* about her new restaurant in Leslieville. It's been the talk of the city all summer. I didn't realize she did private catering too, but money talks, and restaurant margins are thin. Humouring us for the weekend will probably pay bills for the fall. I duck through the far door and find myself wandering through the house, peeking through doorways and around corners, both hopeful and afraid that I will finally be face-to-face with my sister.

She can't really be thinking of selling this place, can she? It would be too easy to wash our hands of everything while the grief is fresh and then regret hasty decisions later. One year. That was the agreement. Then, we'd talk about what to do.

The house is a split level built into the side of the rock. The main floor is flush with the back of the house and the forest beyond, while you can walk out from the lower level under the deck toward the path that leads down to the water.

Sloan is nowhere to be seen on the main level, so I make my way down the stairs. The wine cellar door is open, and the light is on inside. Makes sense that she'd be down here checking on her revenue stream. But when I step inside, the room is silent. I inhale, getting ready for a long sigh. The smell of dust fills my nose. Dad converted this room to be his cellar when I was still small. At first, he'd mostly been into Californian wines. He'd gone to Napa every winter for a month or two, renting a cottage on the backside of some vineyard where he could be left alone to write in peace and work his way through local bottles of chardonnay and cab sauv. Later, his interests had turned to winter vacations to France and the wine regions there. He'd brought home new bottles every year, organizing and reorganizing the shelves in a system he meticulously catalogued. The wine still lies on wooden shelves Dad built himself. A small white tag hangs from each bottle neck. I lift up a few, examining Dad's precise handwriting. *Morrissette des Etoiles. CDR. 2019. Drink ASAP with veal.* The next says *Au Pied du Val. CDR 2020. Rest 5 years.*

On top of the shelf closest to me is a stack of white paper. I take one and find columns of neatly typed details of the auction. *Arnold Fletcher Wine Sale*, says the title. It's a complete inventory of every bottle around me. Maybe two hundred in total. Most are from the last ten years, but there are at least forty from before the turn of the century. 1965. 1977. They have names like Domaine Saint-Arnault and Famille Galipeau. It even includes his notes for when each bottle should be drunk or which should be saved. My throat goes tight. Dad's death may have been cut-and-dried, but it was still sudden. He thought he had more years. Now someone else will get to enjoy his wine.

Before I can get too maudlin, though, voices distract me, coming from somewhere close by. I put the inventory sheet down and pause in the cellar doorway. The lower level isn't as big as upstairs. There's a rec room to my right, a small bathroom to my left, and across, behind the stairs, is the door to what Sloan and I referred to as the dungeon. The room beyond is unfinished, and in some places, the island's rock takes over where the walls leave off. The ceiling is low and it always smells damp. A perfect place to hide a body. That's what we used to say.

But the door is ajar now and light pours through. Inside, two women are having a conversation, and as I creep to the door, I discover it's Sloan and Didi.

"I hope it's enough," Sloan is saying.

"Don't you worry. Vincent will take care of everything," Didi says, her voice all maternal comfort. Sometimes I think Didi pitied us. Poor motherless girls up here all summer with no one to look out for them but Dad, who would sometimes spend days or weeks locked up in his office banging away on his typewriter to craft the words of his latest manuscript. Never mind that our mother was alive and well in Toronto. To Didi's eyes, we were no better than orphans. But while I frequently resented her interference, Sloan always bloomed under the attention.

"Things haven't been good." Sloan's words wobble with unshed tears. "We have six more weeks to make the payment on the property in the Azores or the bank takes it back."

Didi gasps. "They wouldn't do that, would they, sweetheart?"

"And the house in Toronto . . ." Sloan moans. "We should never have put in that three season room, but Bruno said he needed it for inspiration, and that it had to be Tabitha and Luigi who did the plans. They designed the new wing at the Art Gallery of Ontario. And Bruno said it had to be them or it would be a waste of the money he'd borrowed against next year's collection. But then interest rates went up, and he's been so stressed about everything he can't paint. He's behind on deliveries, and now the gallery is threatening to cancel his show this winter. If I can't sell this place, then . . ."

I'm so mad the rest of the conversation fades to silence for a second. Is that what this is about? Fucking Bruno. I never liked him. He's lucky he didn't come this weekend. If he had, I'd have dumped him over the balcony railing and made sure he rolled all the way down to the lake. He and Sloan have no right to use this property as collateral for whatever harebrained vanity project they have going. No doubt Sloan doesn't even plan to split the money from the sale with me. She'll promise to pay me back at some future but unspecified date if I can let them have it all now so she and Bruno can dig themselves out of their self-inflicted hole.

This is it. It's finally time to tell Sloan exactly what I think about all of this and why she's been a shitty sister for months.

But as I take a step forward, from overhead comes a boom so loud the house shakes, followed by the sound of hundreds of running feet. It's a stampede. I hunch instinctively, trying to protect myself from the onslaught, and Sloan and Didi appear at the dungeon door.

"What's going on?" Sloan asks, and I can only shake my head.

Actual footsteps come now, making it clear that what I was hearing wasn't a stampede at all. Still, a lot of people. Some are shouting. Sloan pushes past me, and I follow her back up to the main floor, with Didi close behind. All of the guests are swarming around in the central great room. They're soaked, dripping on the floor and the carpet. Chris and Laurel are clinging to each other. Vincent's white shirt is so drenched I can clearly see the undershirt beneath it.

Outside, the world has turned greenish white. I can't even see the balcony rail through the rain. Up here, it's clear the stampede sound is millions of raindrops pounding down on the roof. Lightning flashes, and the rumble of thunder follows within the same second, making us all jump.

"What's going on?" Sloan asks again. "Is it a tornado?"

One of the Muskoka chairs slams into the floor-to-ceiling window with a bang. A line appears in the glass where it's cracked.

"Maybe we should take a step back," I say.

Another chair, followed by a side table. Its glass top shatters when it hits the window, and the crack in the pane spreads while the furniture is blown out of view again.

"Was this in the forecast?" someone asks, though the storm is so loud now I can't tell who.

"We should get downstairs," I say right before the thunder and lightning come again. They happen simultaneously and we all shout as the house shudders, then plunges into darkness. A woman screams. Even I'm clinging to the closest person, and when my eyes adjust to the shadowy room, I realize I'm wrapped around Amanda's arm.

"You go first," she says, pushing me toward the steps. I didn't even see her when we first came upstairs. I rankle at her telling me what to do, but outside is a wall of water now, and getting low and safe really does feel like the best idea, regardless of whose suggestion it is.

I stumble downstairs again, gripping the railing even as my feet slide on the varnished hardwood stairs. People are rushing behind me, and I have visions of someone slipping and taking us all down like bowling pins. But we manage to get to the basement in one piece. We're all crowded into the space at the bottom, and I get pushed farther away from the stairs. I squeak as the door behind me gives way, sending me tumbling into the wine cellar. My undignified "oof" is muffled by the sound of shattering glass as I collide with a shelf and drop to the floor.

"Who was that?" Sloan asks, though she sounds far away. The inside of the cellar is almost completely dark, too far away from the dim remaining daylight being consumed by the storm outside.

"Are you okay?" It's hard to see her in the dark, but Amanda's voice is unmistakable. She's kneeling next to me, and she's got a hand on my shoulder.

"Fine," I say, going to push myself up and create some space, but the crunch of broken glass under my shoes has me freezing in place. "Shit. I broke a wine bottle."

"What?" Sloan's voice is closer as she pushes through the crowd. "Which one? What did you break? Was it something expensive?"

That *would* be what she's worried about. I roll my eyes, then squint as someone shines a cell phone light in my face. When it moves to the side, Sloan is hovering over me, her gaze on the floor somewhere to my left. She's sucked her bottom lip between her teeth in the way she does when she's thinking hard. A few others have turned on their lights too, and it's enough that I can see around me and safely stand, though I stomp my feet a few times until the broken glass sound goes away.

"Gilly? Honey, are you okay?" Didi appears, stepping between me and Amanda, and now I realize literally everyone is in the wine cellar, and they're all looking at me. I duck my head, trying to escape the glare of lights and curious stares.

"Fine," I say. "I think I avoided the glass."

"Cuvée Saint-Croix," Sloan is saying, still bent over the smashed bottle reading the label. "Is that one of the important ones? Vincent? Is this going to be a problem?"

The cellar gets quiet except for the sound of shuffling feet. The shadows on the walls wheel in different directions as people shine their lights in all the corners. Someone mutters that they have no cell service.

"Vincent?" Sloan asks when no reply comes.

"Vinnie?" Bert adds, in case Vincent has decided he only wants to answer to one and not the other.

"If it's not a 1992, I wouldn't worry too much," the bald man says. He's standing at the far side of the room. In his hand is one of the inventory lists, which he's scanning with serious intensity, holding his flashlight so close to the paper it shines through the other side.

"I think the storm has stopped."

I whirl toward the heavily accented voice. It's not the French man. It's the intimidating ponytail man. Pretty sure it's the first time I've heard him speak since the boat. He's standing closest to the door, one arm draped protectively over the elegant woman. She is drenched and positively shivering.

"Why don't we all go back upstairs?" Didi asks, holding an arm out like a gracious hostess. Our actual hostess is picking at shards of glass like she might be able to put the wine back in the bottle.

Slowly, we emerge from our little hidey-hole. The thunder is farther away, but the staircase is still illuminated periodically by a flash of lightning. In the middle of the line, Laurel squeals, and Chris murmurs something comforting to her. My legs are surprisingly wobbly as I climb. Amanda is behind me. Closer than I want, but not so close I can whirl and tell her to fuck off. We're all on edge. I've been through summer storms before, but never something like that. Understandable that I might be jumpy, but that doesn't mean I can take it out on Amanda or anyone else.

"I think a window is broken," someone says.

"Why is the floor all wet?"

"What about the kitchen staff?"

"Is the power out everywhere?"

"Does anyone else have a cell signal?"

The questions, born of adrenaline and anxiety, tumble out as I reach the top of the stairs. It's still raining, but more in an everyday way, less in a biblical way, and yes, there is definitely a broken—or at least open—window close by, because the floor is slick with—

I scream.

"What? What?"

Heads swivel toward me, and so do a bunch of LED phone flashlights. They don't throw much light, at least not until the others rush toward me, at which point it becomes very clear that the puddle I'm standing in is not water. It's too thick. Too dark.

The blood on my soles is unmistakable, as is the trail it's left on the floor. Wordlessly, the lights follow it, tracing the path until . . .

The body is in the corner of the room, like he's dragged himself there before there was too much blood on the floor and not enough left in him to keep going.

"What's going on? Why the screaming?" Sloan is still coming up the stairs, and ridiculously, I put my finger to my lips and shush her. Not that it matters. The body can't hear her.

Vincent is never going to hear anything again.

# THREE

THE THING about dead bodies is you think you've seen one before. If you've watched TV or seen a movie in the last . . . whenever . . . then your brain believes this is a thing you've done.

True story: it's not, and no matter how much someone might think they're prepared for it, your brain is a lying liar who lies until you're staring at a man you met whose life has now ended on the living room floor where you lost your first tooth thirty-some years ago.

The good news is, if you're not sure what the appropriate reaction is in terms of dealing with an unexpectedly dead body, the group around me has an entire menu of options to choose from. Didi has her hands around her mouth, and silent tears are rolling over her fingertips. Bert has an arm around her, and he's going, "Vinnie? Vinnie?" over and over. The elegant couple from the boat are standing off to one side, looking blank and stoic. Bald man actually works up the guts to nudge Vincent with his toe, which makes Laurel scream. Chris is walking circles around the room holding his phone in the air in the universal motion of trying to find a cell signal.

Sloan says, "But what about the auction?" in a tiny voice. I roll my eyes.

"That's what you're worried about?" I ask. "The auction and your three season room?"

Her gaze flicks to mine and her lips tighten, but before she can reply, Amanda says, "We should call the police." She sounds weirdly calm.

"There's no service," Chris says for probably the fifth time. "Does anyone have service?

The room fills with a general muttering and shuffling as people pull their phones out of their pockets and squint at them. One by one, it becomes apparent that no one has a signal.

"How is that possible?" Laurel asks.

"Don't be ridiculous, of course there's service," Sloan says. "Aren't you always supposed to be able to call 911 from anywhere?"

But we can't. No bars. No connection. Maybe something got knocked down in the storm.

A loud pounding comes from the direction of the kitchen, followed by muffled shouts. The sound makes Laurel shriek again, but Amanda moves quickly, and her take-charge-ness annoys me because this was never her house to begin with and it's not somewhere she's been welcome for years, so she doesn't get to be the one to lead. But she's always had the longest legs of anyone I've ever met, so even as I hurry after her, I can't catch up before she walks through the archway that leads to the dining room and the kitchen beyond and—

"Oh." My heart squeezes as I skid to a halt—or try to skid at least, but my feet slip on the slick floor. This time at least it's water on the hardwood, not blood. The source of it is the gaping wound in the ceiling where a giant pine tree has crashed through, smashing the windows and crushing the dining room table. Water drips from the opening. Beyond the tangle of branches, the deck railing has been destroyed as the giant tree toppled over, but beyond that, it's hard to make out the extent of the damage.

"Hello?" The banging comes again. "Hello? Is anyone out there?"

"Kitchen," Amanda says.

It takes some work. A branch is pressed up against the door, trapping the staff inside. By the time we've pulled it free, my hands are sticky with sap and I smell like a forest, but finally, the door is open wide enough for Reena and her frightened cooks to stumble out and see the rest of the damage.

"Everything okay in there?" Amanda asks, nodding toward the kitchen.

Reena says, "Yes. Power's out, but the gas on the stove still works. You?"

"Fine," I say.

"Except for the dead body!" someone calls from the other room.

"Dead body?" one of the cooks asks. Slowly, we pick our way back to the living room.

"Was someone hurt?" Reena asks.

"You could say that," Chris says with an arch of his eyebrow. Laurel swats at him and he goes back to walking around with his phone in the air trying to find a signal.

"Was it a heart attack?" Didi asks.

"There's so much blood," Bert says. "Vinnie? Are you okay?"

"Looks like someone hit him in the back of the head." This is from the bald man. "Maybe with a stick or a wine bottle?"

I don't know much about these kinds of things, but his assessment seems plausible. Vincent is lying face down on the ground. The back of his head is matted with blood that's pooling and spreading along the floorboards.

"A wine bottle?" Sloan asks. "Which one? Was it expensive?"

"I don't know." He turns in a circle. "The bottle isn't here."

"Who are you, exactly?" I ask the bald man.

He stands up straight puffing out his chest. "My name is Jean-Guy Closson."

Behind him, Chris snorts. "He's the number one wine journalist in Europe. How can you not have heard of him?"

"Why would I have heard of him?" I say, bristling.

"Who are *you*, anyway?" Laurel asks, coming to stand next to Chris. She tips her chin up at an angle that says exactly what she thinks of me.

"She's my sister," Sloan says wearily.

"Sister?" Laurel pales. She's clearly thinking about how she shit-talked my dad's book and tried to gossip about his death.

Sloan doesn't have time for family trees. "Can we please get back to the question of what we do with the dead body on my floor?"

"Your floor?" I ask. "*Your* floor? If anything, it's our floor."

"Now really isn't the time, Gilly." She glances around nervously. She loves an audience, but not when it's her bad behaviour that's being called out.

"When would have been the time?" I ask, voice rising. She can't run away this time. With everyone watching, I can pin her down like a bug in a collection and make her listen. "After the funeral? Because I thought we were in agreement back then. Or when you hired Barney and Meredith to design your three season room? Would it have been any one of the dozen times I've called? Or when I emailed? Or texted? When would be the right time to talk about the fact you're selling the house out from under me? This is my home too, Sloan!"

As I finish speaking, my throat hurts from shouting, and my ears are hot. The room is silent except for the sound of wind in the trees and water dripping through the hole in the roof. Everyone is watching, and meanwhile, the dead auctioneer is still lying motionless on the floor behind Bert and Didi with a growing wine-red blood pool around his head.

"Who are Barney and Meredith?" Sloan asks, sounding genuinely confused. "We hired Tabitha and Luigi."

She doesn't get it.

"Oh, I love them," Laurel says. "The extension on the AGO is so beautiful."

For fuck's sake. I can't deal with any of this. Not Sloan. Not the house. Not the Tabitha and Luigi fan club. Not even the dead guy on the floor.

I spin on my heel and storm out.

Or I try. The sliding door to the living room is jammed, and I have to throw my whole weight into it to get it open. Outside, the railing is smashed, but the portion of the deck closest to me is sturdy enough I can find my way down to the steps, which are covered in branches and leaves but still in one piece.

I walk a careful path to the water. I don't know where I'm going, really. The sun is halfway down now, and the sky is already dark from the storm. The whole lake is so quiet it's eerie. Not a single boat on the water, no lights on at any of the few cottages that are visible from the end of the dock. In fact, Bert and Didi's cottage isn't visible at all. Their island is a mess of broken trees, and their boathouse is leaning wildly to one side.

Speaking of Bert and Didi . . .

"Shit."

Their boat is gone. The white sailboat that was here when Murray pulled up. The lines are still looped around the cleats on the dock and dangling in the water. They must have snapped in the storm. Not the only boat to have been forcibly relocated. Someone's kayak has washed up on the small gravel beach next to the dock. It's a nice one. Or it was, I guess. Handmade, probably, from long strips of wood. Now it's been smashed to kindling.

"Gillian!"

I hurry to wipe the frustrated tears from my cheeks as Amanda comes down the dock, her feet echoing on the wet wood.

"I don't really feel like talking to you," I say, hunching in on myself. The temperature has dropped a good ten degrees since before the storm, but the humidity still hangs in the air, leaving a cool slick against my skin.

"Where are you going?" she asks.

"For a swim." Farther out on the lake, a loon emerges. It's got a wriggling fish in its bill, and it tips its head back, swallowing the whole thing in one go. The bird seems completely oblivious to the devastation around it, and I'm envious. I can't even decide what the bigger problem is at the moment—my sister or the dead auctioneer.

"We have to call for help," Amanda says, coming to stand beside me. She's clearly aware my threat of going swimming is an empty one.

I check my phone. No signal. I dial 911 anyway, but nothing happens, so I show her the phone for a second before I wordlessly stuff it back in my pocket. She nods.

"It's the same up there," she says, nodding toward the house. "Is there a radio anywhere?"

I hadn't thought of a radio.

"On the boat," I say. "This way."

Not that she needs me to lead her. She knows where the boathouse is. Ours is in better shape than Bert and Didi's. It's missing a few shingles, but none of the windows are broken. It takes a little effort to convince the door to open, but that's not unusual. It always used to swell with the summer heat and humidity.

What isn't normal is the absence of a boat inside.

"What the . . ." I let the question trail off. The closed doors that lead out to the water mean it didn't break loose and drift away in the storm. In fact, the closed doors should have been my first clue that something was wrong. We never leave them closed during the boating season. It's way too much of a pain to get them open and closed from inside a bobbing boat.

Which means . . .

"Son of a bitch," I mutter.

"What?" Amanda's standing beside me, hands on her hips.

"Sloan," I say. "She probably sold the boat. Why else would Murray have to ferry us all over here?" I throw in a few choice words because what the hell? Sloan was always more of a sunbather than a boater. She didn't like wearing hats or the way the wind would mess up her hair. Obviously the first thing she would do is get rid of the boat. I hope she got a good price for it at least. It was a vintage Chris-Craft that Dad restored when we were in high school. It would have been worth a good chunk of money. At least half a three season room. A season and a half.

Anger rises up like a thundercloud inside me again. I push past Amanda before she can react. I shouldn't have walked away before. I wasn't in control of my emotions and needed space to think, and instead, all it's done is solidify how much Sloan is only here to dismantle our childhood board by board.

"Gilly, wait!" Amanda's coming after me again.

"Fuck off," I say, not looking back.

"No. Wait. Before you go up there, I have to—"

I duck under a low-hanging branch that's snapped off one of the other massive pine trees on the property. My head brushes against the needles, and water slithers inside my shirt and down my spine.

I say, "We're not together anymore. You don't have to do anything except stay away from me."

"No, but—"

I have one foot on the bottom step when she grabs me.

"Let go!" I say, but instead of doing that she wraps an arm around my chest and backs us up. I stumble over my feet and squeak when she claps a hand over my mouth. What the hell? Did she come here after all these years to kidnap me?

"Quiet." She's pulled us behind a rosebush planted at the bottom of the steps. Crouched down as we are, it's taller than us. Also, I'm fully soaked now. Water is seeping through my pants where I'm kneeling on the moist ground. She's got us pressed tight together, her cheek against mine. Once upon a time, this would have been romantic, but now, I'm even angrier than I was a minute ago. I struggle, but of course, since she's got seven inches on me and I never did wind up training to run the marathon I said I would with all the free time I suddenly had after our breakup, I don't have the strength to do much besides grind my knees further into the mud.

"Shh," she whispers in my ear. "Listen."

I don't want to listen to anything she has to say. But through the haze of my frustration comes the sound of angry voices overhead. I still, straining to listen. A man and a woman, though the conversation is mostly whispers, so it's hard to hear what they're saying.

Amanda hushes me again, and this time, I nod. She lets me go, and I lean forward so I can see beyond the edge of the deck, looking upward. It's the man and woman from the boat. Slick ponytail man and his regal companion. Even if we can't hear the words—or understand them, since they weren't speaking English tearlier and I assume they still aren't—whatever's going on is not a friendly conversation. She's stabbing at his chest with a pointed finger while he argues back, muttering in low tones that make me shiver. He's clearly not a man who likes to be argued with, but whoever they are to each other, she doesn't care.

Amanda taps the back of my hand and slips back to her hiding place under the deck. She puts a finger to her lips and motions me to follow. The whole thing of us scuttling under the structure of the deck and ducking our heads to avoid banging them on the support beams reminds me of childhood days spent playing capture the flag, and Amanda takes it as seriously now as Sloan and I did back then.

But why?

"What are you doing?" I whisper to her as the voices of the couple overhead fade.

"I need to tell you something."

We're reaching the far end of the deck. There's a path that runs along the side of the house, and beyond is a shed that used to hold various summer activity equipment. Life jackets and fishing poles. It's leaning precariously now, but it stays upright when Amanda yanks the door open.

"Why are you being weird?" I ask, but when she shushes me again, I roll my eyes and step inside. She follows, pulling the door nearly closed so that only a thin sliver of the dying light filters in. I'm immediately consumed with the idea of a million spiders watching us from the corners. Anytime I came in here to get something, I was guaranteed to put my hand on a daddy longlegs first.

"We have to find a way to contact the police," Amanda says.

"I'm open to suggestions," I say. "The phones aren't working. Murray's coming to get me in the morning. People are squeamish, but the best we can do is ignore the dead body on the floor, call it an early night or drink what we want out of the cellar, and hope Murray's got a radio tomorrow."

She pauses. I don't need more light to identify the expression she's making. It's the one she'd make after a difficult phone call from work. It's the one where she wanted to call the person on the phone every name in the book but instead went with, "Well, if that's what you think, I guess I'll be on a plane tomorrow."

Now, she says, "What do you think happened to that man on the floor?"

I shrug. I hadn't really thought about it, to be honest. Probably did my best to not think about it at all. But since she's asking, I give it my best guess.

"He was hit by the falling tree?" I don't mean to say it like a question, but that's how it comes out.

Amanda lets out a long exhale through her nose. "Really?"

What am I supposed to say? "Are you telling me you know what happened?" I ask. What even is going on? She's being weird, but now, apprehension tickles over my skin, like maybe the weirdness has a purpose.

Another exhale. This time, I'm the one she's silently calling every name in the book.

"Don't freak out, okay?" she says.

"I'd be less freaked out if you'd stop with all the cloak-and-dagger bullshit." This is why we broke up. This, right here. Because she'd never give me a straight answer about anything. There'd be a lot of smiling and vague staring off into the distance. Silent acknowledgements that she'd heard my question but wasn't planning to respond. Or else she'd say something like, "We'll talk when I get back," which entirely defeated the point of my plaintive, "But why do you have to go at all?"

"It wasn't the tree," she says. "And you know that."

"Don't tell me what I do and don't—" My voice rises, and she cuts me off with another furious *shh* and a finger to my lips. I smack her hand away but don't say anything. We're way too close inside the small shed.

"He was killed, Gil," she says, and the short form of my

name makes heat rise up on the back of my neck. My head is a mess. It has been since I got in the car this morning and started driving north, and now I can't keep track which way is up and whether I'm mad at Amanda for being here or want her to press me up against the plywood and kiss me until everything is normal again for a minute. I guess I'll have to settle for her hand on my shoulder as she says, "Murdered. Do you understand?"

I snort. "What do you mean murdered? Who's going to murder him?"

"The people on the deck, I think," she says, without a hint of humor, which makes it awkward when I giggle. I wipe my lips with my hand and force myself to be serious, then fail immediately.

"What? Boris and Natasha up there?"

She makes an exasperated noise. "His name is Yuriy Sobal. He's a banker for organized crime in Eastern Europe."

That has the next laugh dying in my throat. I squint, though it's getting harder and harder to see her at all in the dwindling light.

"What?" I say.

"I'm not kidding, Gilly."

No. It doesn't sound like she is. The apprehension in my spine turns to alarm bells in my head.

"And what?" I say slowly. "He's a banker for organized crime and his wife is a mafia princess with a fondness for fine wine?"

"Lana, a former Russian ballerina turned choreographer."

"Oh." A small relief.

"But yes. There's a strong indication her family also has ties to oligarchs and war criminals in Russia and Belarus."

"Jesus Christ."

She makes a noise of agreement. "I know."

"No, I mean, Jesus Christ, what are you saying?" The giggle

finally breaks free. "You show up out of the blue and expect me to believe some bullshit story about murder and organized crime in the Muskokas? You really are a piece of work, aren't you? Forget it, Amanda. Swap ghost stories with someone else."

I go to storm out of the shed. At least I'm confident the door will open this time, but she catches my wrist.

"Listen!" she says, and for the first time her cool composure cracks. "It's not safe. Listen to me."

"Let go. Why would I believe you? How could you possibly know that? You don't travel in the same circles." I smack at her hand, but her grip might as well be a handcuff for all the progress I make.

"We do, in fact," she says through gritted teeth.

"What? Have you been investing for Toronto mob bosses on the side?"

"No. Gilly. Stop. Just listen."

"Why?" I say, and suddenly we're back on the deck six years ago as she begged me to listen and I didn't. I was done. Hurt. Heartbroken. Just like now.

"This is important. If they've already killed one person here, they won't stop if anyone else gets in their way."

"You're not making any sense." But even as I argue, the back of my mind is replaying the moments right before I stepped in the pool of blood. The cellar. The storm. Yuriy and Lana standing by the door, drenched. Were they so wet because they stayed upstairs after the tree fell to bludgeon Vincent to death? That can't be possible, right? "What are you even saying? Why are you here?"

"Because it's my job," she says.

"You're a banker," I say.

"I'm not. You know I'm not. You knew then too." She pulls me toward her. I don't want to go, but it feels like the world is falling out from beneath my feet and the only way to keep from dropping into nothingness is to stick close to her. She sighs as I press against her chest, squeezing my eyes shut. "You were always too smart. I was in so much trouble from the day I met you."

It almost sounds like an apology. Years too late. I hold on to her tighter.

"What's going on?" I ask.

Her sigh might as well suck every inch of air from her body, but somehow, she has enough to say the words I have no reason to believe but have been expecting since the last time I walked away from her.

"I'm not just a banker. Never was. It's a cover, Gil. I work in intelligence."

*You were always too smart.* Right now, though, I don't feel very intelligent.

"Say it again," I whisper. "In very small words."

"I'm a spy," she says. "And we're in danger."

# FOUR

TO SUM UP, here's the situation as I understand it (though my understanding is changing by the minute):

My sister has invited a bunch of strangers to the house to sell off my dad's wine collection before she sells the rest of the house out from under me.

There's a hole in the roof, a fallen tree in the dining room, and a dead man on the living room floor.

The aforementioned dead man has nothing to do with the tree or the hole but does, apparently, have to do with the mob banker and his evil ballerina bride, who may or may not be here to buy wine.

And my ex-girlfriend is a spy.

Somehow, that's the least shocking revelation of the evening.

I burst back outside. I can't breathe. After Amanda's truth bomb, the walls of the shed had started to close in. A slow rain is falling again, and fat raindrops drip through the deck and splatter on my neck and shoulders.

"I knew it," I mutter over and over. "I knew it. I knew it."

"Shh," Amanda says, following after me.

I jab a finger in her direction. "You were always keeping things from me."

Feet sound overhead. Amanda is standing a small distance away, looking upward. I imagine her in a black leather catsuit, her hip cocked as she plants a booted foot on the ground, gun raised.

My ex-girlfriend is a super spy.

And I am pissed off. It's leftover anger from being so close to Sloan, but now I direct it at Amanda instead.

"What the hell?" I growl at her, doing my best to keep my voice down. "What do you mean? You're a banker."

She winces. "Officially, the term is wealth manager."

I throw my hands up in the air. "Same difference, Amanda!" Honestly, I never understood what she did. She tried to explain it a few times, but when she used words like acquisitions and equity, my brain would go to mush, and I stopped listening.

But maybe it never made sense because it wasn't true. What if she made it sound as boring as the fine art of mixing white paint so I'd stop asking questions?

The chronicle of our time together is retelling itself. Only now, instead of my poised, sophisticated, wealthy girlfriend at my back, it's a secret agent. All those nights at events. What were we doing there?

I glare at her. "You have some explaining to do."

She nods, lips thin. "Later. Right now, there's a good chance we're in danger and need to find a way off this island before—"

Overhead, raised voices sound.

"What do you mean?" a woman says.

"This is unacceptable. What kind of auction is this?"

"I never agreed to—"

"Please, if you would—" Sloan starts to say, but she gets cut off in a babble of angry protests. Whatever they've been up to, tensions are rising. The deck creaks ominously. Half a tree is leaning over the far side, and one of the beams that keeps the structure upright is warped, bowing in the middle.

I tug on Amanda's sleeve. The last thing I need right now is to get crushed by a collapsing deck. The good news, at least as I see it, is that the storm damage and the dead body mean Sloan can't sell the whole thing anymore. At least not right away. But we'll have even bigger problems if these people all tumble to their deaths on top of everything, so I climb back up the wreckage of the stairs and hurry to where Sloan is pinned up against the railing by angry wine enthusiasts. Bert and Didi have planted themselves in front of her and are arguing loudly with the others. Chris and Laurel are closest, but the French journalist is turning a weird shade of purple as he shoves at Bert's chest. Two of the kitchen staff are also involved. Amanda's mobster is not. He and the murder ballerina are standing close to the door that leads back into the living room, almost like they're guarding their kill. They watch me suspiciously, then as a pair, their gazes slide to Amanda as she comes up the stairs behind me.

"Do they know about you?" I whisper quietly to her. Over the shouting near the rail, there's no way I can be overheard.

She makes a face that would be hilariously comical if it weren't for the current circumstances.

"I certainly hope not. I wouldn't be very good at my job if they did."

So many questions. *Is* she good at her job? What exactly is her job? Who does she work for? Everything I know about spies I learned from watching TV and movies. But she's Canadian. We don't have the FBI or the CIA. Here it's CSIS and . . . what? The RCMP? Is my ex-girlfriend a Mountie? I didn't know people lied about being Mounties. They're basically the Canadian poster child. But what if that's a front? What if the red coats and big hats hide some top-secret shit that no one's supposed to know about?

More importantly, Chris has pushed past Bert and looks like he's about to throw my sister over the railing. It's a long way down, and even though I'm still mad at her, I don't want her getting hurt.

"Hey," I say, elbowing my way forward through the crowd. "What's going on? Hey, stop." I grab Chris's arm, and he whirls so fast I stumble, tripping over my own feet before crashing to the ground. The commotion rises again. Sloan says my name like she might actually be worried about me, but it's Amanda who creates enough space for me to stand.

"That's enough," she's saying. "Arguing won't accomplish anything."

"Then what will?" Laurel asks. Her makeup is running down teary cheeks, mirroring the expression of a lot of the people around us. Sloan's gone pale, and Didi is huddled against Bert, who has a protective arm over her shoulder. The French reporter's face is still mottled, but the anger is slowly transforming into fear. The kitchen staff have regrouped, with Reena positioned protectively in front of them like she might have to fight off a bear or something.

The only people not in our immediate vicinity are Yuriy and Lana. They're standing in the doorway, speaking quietly to each other and glancing inside the house from time to time. My heart picks up and my throat goes dry. What do killers look like? Probably like everyone else. If they wore little name tags or windbreakers that said Murder and Mayhem for Hire," they wouldn't get very far.

And now we're stuck here with them.

"There has to be a way off the island," Laurel is saying, echoing my thoughts.

"There isn't," I say. I can't help myself when I throw a glare in Sloan's direction. "Dad's boat got sold." That she won't meet my gaze is all the confirmation I need.

"What about the Minuet?" Bert says. "We were going to sail home after supper."

I shake my head. "Lines snapped in the storm. I'm sorry, Bert. The boat is gone."

Yuriy steps toward us, and I flinch, reaching for Amanda's hand without meaning to. I'm annoyed when she gives me a reassuring squeeze, so I snatch it back, fumbling for a pocket that isn't there, before awkwardly clutching my wrist to my chest like I meant to do that all along.

For a killer, his smile is surprisingly kind. He says, "I'm sorry, but is it possible to have something to eat?" His English is very accented, but the question is still clear.

So of course all I can think to stammer out in reply is, "Wh-what?"

The lines around his mouth are tight as he gives me an apologetic smile and says, "My wife. She is diabetic, and we've had a long day. She needs something to eat."

My gaze slides past him to where Lana is still standing in the door. She has the same tension at the corners of her lips, and where before her hand on the doorframe looked like the graceful pose of a dancer aware of her limbs at all times, now it looks like she really does need the support.

"Oh, you poor dear," Didi says.

"I'm so sorry," Sloan rushes forward, going back into hostess mode. "There should have been dinner by now."

I can't help myself when I say, "Pretty hard to serve dinner when the dining room is destroyed." The remark earns me a variety of confused and annoyed looks from the assembled guests and staff, as well as a cleared throat and a gentle bump of my hip from Amanda. I take a step away from her. Banker or spy, she's not my girlfriend. She doesn't get to tell me what to do.

Keep the criminals fed, survive until morning, and get off the island. That's my to-do list.

Soon enough, we're all lounging around the kitchen island and munching on what was cooked before the power went out. I can't quite find somewhere comfortable to stand. At first, I hop up on one of the stools near the fridge, but when Amanda joins me, I hop down just as fast, ignoring the look she gives me. Bert and Didi are talking with Sloan by the front windows, and I'm no longer in the mood to talk to Sloan. Yuriy has dragged a pair of chairs from the dining room in for himself and Lana, and it's not like I'd want to sit with them anyway. In the end, I wind up lingering by the door to the back hall, eating skewers of cherry tomatoes and halloumi cheese.

"Should we open a bottle of wine?" Chris asks hopefully. No one laughs, and his hope dims. The conversations are muted. The cooks are all clustered together, poking at plates of food too. Sloan keeps throwing them looks like she's unhappy to be eating with the help, even though if you showed a hundred people on the streets of Toronto pictures of Sloan and Reena, I have no doubt they'd recognize Reena before my sister.

I watch Yuriy and Lana. Like they have been since we arrived, they've got their heads together and are talking quietly without acknowledging the presence of other people in the room. Are they really what Amanda said? If they killed Vincent, they're definitely keeping a low profile now, which I guess would make sense, since they're as trapped as the rest of us. The best option is to wait until morning and hope they can sneak away. After a few minutes, Lana does sit up straighter and smiles more as Yuriy speaks, so his story about her being unwell and needing to eat checks out at least.

I'm so focused on them that I don't notice until it's too late as the plate I'm holding dips, and the last skewer of cheese and tomatoes rolls until it lands on my chest with a splat. A smear of balsamic vinegar darkens my shirt, and this really is the very least of my problems, but all I can do is let out a loud sigh that has everyone looking toward me.

"Excuse me," I say, ducking into the hall. I curse as I undo the buttons. Not like I have anything to change into here. But I need a second to think, and scrubbing stains out of my shirt gives me that.

Except there's no water. No power means the pump to the well isn't working, and when I turn the tap on in the bathroom, nothing happens. I hold my hand under the faucet like that might help, but of course, it doesn't. This whole situation is chaos.

In the dim silence of the bathroom, voices reach me from further up the hall. They're whispered and hurried, and I can't make out what they're saying. Is someone there? Who wasn't in the kitchen? It only takes a few steps up the hall before the words start to make sense.

"We had an agreement. And this wasn't it," a woman's voice says. My pulse picks up at the thought it might be Sloan.

"I didn't think it would happen this way." It's the journalist. The most important one in France or Europe or wherever. Why can't I remember his name?

"With him dead?" No, not Sloan. The woman is Laurel, clearly trying to keep herself under control so she can't be heard. "No one said anything about him dying."

"It's the perfect opportunity." Unlike her, the man's voice is cool. Calculating. I'm standing in the middle of the hall and something tells me to hide, even though I can't see them. They're in one of the guest rooms, and I duck into the one across the hall, sliding myself behind the door.

"But Chris," Laurel says, and the words are tight. "If he ever finds out . . ."

"We have already talked about how you can handle him."

My palms prickle. I lean forward, straining to hear, and the door swings forward too. Desperately, I try to catch it, but my nails slide uselessly against the wood, only pushing it faster, until it shuts with a gentle thump. I freeze, squeezing my eyes tight. The voices are gone, but I can't tell if it's because they overheard me or the door has muffled their conversation too much.

"Laurel?" Chris's voice comes from the direction of the kitchen. "Babe?"

"I'm getting a sweater!" Laurel answers. Then one set of footsteps sounds in the hall, the floorboards creaking. I stay where I am, even though my heart is doing everything it can to exit through my throat and make a break for it.

Feed the criminals. Stay alive until morning. Get help.

What if we've been feeding the wrong criminals?

# FIVE

AFTER WHAT SEEMS LIKE FOREVER, a second set of footsteps comes, trailing back toward the main part of the house. I'm still plastered against the door, holding my breath. What am I supposed to do? If I come back through the kitchen, there will be no question which way I came from. If Laurel and the journalist know I overheard them, does that make me next on their hit list?

The window in this room faces the back of the house and a dense forest that has, at different times in my life, seemed menacing and protective. Since the house is built onto a slope, this side is much closer to ground level. I push the window up and pull the screen aside. It's still a bit of a drop, but the soft soil takes my weight without more than a slight twinge in my ankle.

I go around to the water side of the house and climb the deck stairs. Despite my fears, no one seems to pay much attention to me as I make my way back into the kitchen. Sloan's found some candles, and the whole room flickers in their flames. Chris and Laurel are standing together once again. The journalist lingers in the shadows by the back hall.

"Hey." I tug at Amanda's sleeve. She's installed by the door to the dining room, observing everyone. Is this what she did before? All those nights we were moving and shaking with the Toronto who's who? She could talk to anyone, effortlessly folding people into our conversation. Was she thinking the whole time? Looking for inconsistencies in stories? Building relationships with targets so it would be easier to track their movements and business activities afterward?

She gives me a startled glance. "Where did you come from?"

I shake my head, drawing her through the door. The clouds have parted, and stars twinkle down on us through the hole in the roof. The fallen tree is a prickly shape that we have to make our way around and under before we're in the living room. The house is quiet, the sounds of conversations in the kitchen muffled. My phone still has no signal, but the flashlight works, and I turn it on to light our way. The body is still on the floor by the stairs. Someone's draped a beach towel over him. I recognize it—bright blue with a lime green sea turtle. Its presence on the motionless form is familiar and also deeply weird.

"What's going on?" Amanda says.

"How sure are you that the Russians killed him?" I ask, waving my light toward the dead man.

"They're Belarusian," she says, then seems to remember that's not relevant to my question. "Or Yuriy is, at least. Why? Did he say something to you?"

I shake my head. "No, but I think I heard the real killers talking."

I relay what I overheard between Laurel and the journalist. I talk quickly and in whispers, like someone might jump out of the shadows at any moment, gun drawn. They'll tell me I know too much, and they're sorry it had to end this way.

Except that doesn't actually happen, does it? Not in real life. This is Canada, for god's sake. People don't walk around with guns. And if they did, why didn't they use it on the auctioneer?

But Amanda must be thinking along the same lines, because she glances around before pulling her own phone out and using the light to guide us down the stairs back to the wine cellar where she carefully closes the door. She does a careful walk around the room like she's checking for eavesdroppers—or perhaps for listening devices?—before she turns her attention back to me.

"Okay, tell me again exactly what you heard."

I do. Or I try. Already the details are fading. Human memory is so crap.

"Did she say what the agreement was?" Amanda asks.

"She said—" I struggle. Did she? "She said Chris couldn't know."

"But did she actually say she'd killed him?"

When I open my mouth to answer, nothing comes out at first.

"They know something," I say, scrambling for answers. "About him. Something no one else knows."

"Something they'd kill him for?"

I scrunch my face tight as embarrassment creeps over the back of my neck. I've overreacted. Not my fault. The whole day has been emotionally charged, and coming across the two of them in the hall was the icing on the paranoia cake.

"I'm sorry," I say, hanging my head. "I'm seeing suspects everywhere. They're probably having an affair or something."

"No, it's definitely a possibility," Amanda says.

I grimace. "He's a lot older than she is."

"No, I mean it's definitely possible they killed him."

"What?" My head snaps up as the question echoes off the walls. Good thing we're downstairs.

Now it's her turn to scrunch her face up sheepishly. "Yuriy's capable of it, but killing someone like this in a public way leaves them vulnerable, especially in a foreign country. Whatever they're doing here, they'll want an easy exit, and being murder suspects complicates that."

"Then why did you tell me they killed him?" I ask.

"I'm not saying they didn't. Complicated isn't impossible. It may have been an opportunistic thing. Or they didn't realize the storm would trap us all here until it was too late to reverse course. But if it's the journalist and the woman . . ." She's pacing now. "Do you know anything else about them?"

"Not really?"

"You all came on the boat together. Did they seem like they met before? Were they friendly?"

"Are you asking if they're having an affair?"

She shrugs. "Wouldn't be the most off-the-wall hypothesis."

"That doesn't make sense. If they're sleeping together in secret, wouldn't they pretend to be strangers?"

"Couples sleep with each other's friends all the time."

That comment brings me up short because the question that follows is, does she? Or did she when we were a couple? If she wasn't honest about what she did for a living, what else didn't she tell me?

But like she already has a few times tonight, she seems to understand exactly what I'm thinking, because she squeezes my hand.

"Hey," she says. "Not like that. Never, and definitely not while we were together. You were it for me, and then you told me to leave."

Her words make mine catch in my throat on something that feels suspiciously like tears. I was angry with her for a long time. I was the one who called it quits, but even so, there was never any closure. No answers to the secrets she was keeping. And now I have them—or some of them, anyway—and it's left me even more off-balance than ever.

When I don't answer, she lets my hand go with a nod like

she's got some new answers of her own. I should apologize, though for what exactly is unclear.

She says, "Okay, let's take a step back. Everyone is a suspect."

"It wasn't me," I say. "I was the first one down the stairs when the storm hit."

She nods. "Who else? Who came down after you?"

I struggle to remember. Sloan? She was closest to me. But when I was running back to the stairs, she was still playing hostess and running toward the others. And then it was a big tumble of limbs and bodies into the dark. Even if Yuriy and Lana were closest to the door when everything was over, that doesn't mean the killer didn't push past them. No way to say for sure who was there last. It took a minute or more before anyone even noticed Vincent wasn't there. Lots of time for the group to move around.

"I saw them talking," I say, as a memory finally pops into view.

"Who?"

"Vincent and the journalist. On the deck before the storm. Vincent didn't seem happy about whatever it was the journalist had to say."

She nods eagerly. "That's good. That's a possible motive. We have to find out what it is."

I can't help my grin. "Like investigate this? Does that make me a spy?"

She sighs. "There's more to it than that. And it's not all it's cracked up to be. It's a lot of paperwork. And meetings. So many meetings."

"Spies have meetings?"

"More like I sit in on other people's meetings. I spent two days trying not to fall asleep in an IMF summit last year and—" She cocks her head.

"And?" For the first time since I pulled up in the boat, I might be about to enjoy myself.

"Shit," she hisses as her gaze snaps to mine. "I'm really sorry."

"About what?" I ask. Or try to. Before I can get it all out, she's crowding up against me, walking me backward until I collide with a wine rack. Bottles clink together. Amanda mutters another apology, but I still don't get a chance to find out what for before her mouth is coming down on mine.

Oh. Probably this.

Not that I mind.

Much.

Kissing Amanda has always been easy. From that first night at the gala, finding her mouth in the dark and forgetting the world around me was the simplest thing in the world. Apparently, that hasn't changed. Neither has the way I instinctively start pulling at her, trying to bring her closer, even as the bottles rattle behind us. It's been six years, and no one lights me up like she does. I remember everything about this, from her taste to the way she settles her hands on my hips, holding me close.

"Slap me," she says in my ear, voice breathy.

That's certainly new.

"What?"

"Slap me. As soon as—"

A gust of air blows through the room as the door swings open. Amanda rips herself back, stumbling like she's been pushed, and at the last second, I follow, swinging my hand until it smacks across her cheek. I wince at the impact, then at her surprised expression as she touches the place I hit.

Which is nothing compared to the shock on Didi's face as I finally notice her over Amanda's shoulder.

"Oh. Oh my." Her own hand is on her cheek like she's the

one who's been slapped. "I'm sorry. Bert told me—" The corner of her mouth turns up in a bemused smile. "If you two are—"

"We're not," I say. Amanda is still close, so I push her away —gently, but she sells it again—and make my escape. "Excuse me."

The whole way up the stairs, I can feel their eyes on the back of my neck. My nerves are on fire. I haven't exactly been a nun since Amanda and I broke up, but it's not like women have been falling at my feet either. I've been on dates, but the apps are a horror, and sometimes it's like I've already met every lesbian in Toronto. So there have been dates, and even one sloppy make-out session at Pride a couple of years ago, but lately my love life has been quiet. I've missed having someone to touch. Someone to kiss.

And Amanda always was a very good kisser.

But it doesn't matter. That won't be happening again. It shouldn't have happened the first time. Blame adrenaline. Anxiety. We broke up because she wouldn't tell me the truth, but now that she has, we're not on any firmer footing than we were back then. A spy? What does that even mean? I have too many questions and no time to deal with them. There's still a killer in the house, and Murray's coming in twelve hours to take me away. I'll never have to see Amanda again, and that's for the best.

I stumble at the top of the stairs, and a phone flashlight swings in my direction. It's Sloan, standing near the body.

"Guess you'll have to get the blood stain off the flooring before you can convince someone to buy the place," I say.

She twists her lips and, for a second, looks like she's going to walk away. Instead, she says, "He was my dad too. In case you forgot."

It's so unexpected that I freeze on the spot, standing in the dark room. We're like gunslingers about to have a standoff, except we're armed with flashlights instead of pistols.

When I say nothing, she looks down at the body on the floor again, shaking her head. Sloan sighs and says something like, "Now what are we going to do?" Outside, there's a rumble of fresh thunder and a flash of lightning. Sloan flinches and turns her attention back to me. "Was there something you wanted? Besides telling me I'm a shitty sister?"

Was there? Now that we're face-to-face, I can't remember. An unexpected surge of sympathy wells up in me. I've been so mad at her since I found out she was trying to sell the house, but the sadness in her eyes now is the same deep grief that's been eating at me for months. We lost our dad. Didn't even get a chance to say goodbye. That's going to hurt for a long time. Possibly forever.

Some instinct says to tell her what Amanda and I have been talking about. That she should know what happened. It's not like Sloan killed him. Or did she? The thought chills me, and I brush it aside as quickly as it popped up.

I ask, "How well do you know the other guests? Who made the cut?"

"I don't," she says. "They were friends of Vincent's and Bert's. Tonight, anyway. Bert said that was the way things were usually done. VIPs get invited for a preview. I have some friends coming tomorrow. Taffy and Alexa. Remember them?"

I don't. And it's really not the point. What she's saying is one of Vincent's own friends killed him.

"Didi?" Bert's voice comes from behind the tree in the dining room. "Everything okay out there?"

"Coming!" Didi appears at the top of the stairs, a wine bottle in each hand. Amanda is behind her, looking serious. Didi tiptoes around us. Sloan gives me a final glance and follows her. The room is dark again except for the puddle of light around my feet where my phone shines. A pair of shoes are a few inches from mine, connected to Vincent's motionless legs. It's still weird to me that I don't feel much looking down at him, other than vague amusement about the turtle towel.

"I guess you see these often," I say as Amanda comes to stand next to me.

"What?"

"Dead bodies."

She snorts. "I told you, it's not like that. You were there. It's a lot of small talk. My job is to gather intelligence, not kill people."

That makes me feel both better and worse. I was there. And I never saw it. The fight has gone out of me, though. With her. With Sloan. I shouldn't have come. I was mad at my sister, and now, I've made an ass of myself and kissed Amanda, which is, frankly, still messing with my head.

"I'm going to sleep in the boathouse," I say. "Please don't follow me or wake me up unless someone else dies."

I'm about to lift the phone to guide my way out to the deck, but at the last second, a flash of white catches my attention. Just a reflection on the pool of congealed blood and wine. Or was it? I swing the beam back down, and the white triangle amid the dark is too sharp to be a reflection.

"What's wrong?" Amanda asks as I bend, trying not to grimace when I pull the rectangular card from the cool, sticky goo on the floor. Most of it is hidden beneath Vincent's leg, and the part of me that still thinks we're in a TV show says I shouldn't disturb the body. That the police will want to see him exactly as we found him. But someone else has already contaminated the crime scene with the towel. Poking around by his feet won't change that he's dead or that someone killed him. And Amanda can vouch for me.

Unless Amanda killed him . . .

I freeze halfway back to standing as the thought occurs to me. She said she's not that kind of spy, but how can I be sure that's true? Not when she's lied about everything else. What if she's expecting me to vouch for her when she's the one who killed him the whole time?

"Gil?" Her hand on my spine makes me jump, and I straighten, hoping my hands don't shake.

"Nothing," I say.

"Looks like something." She's talking about the card in my hand, not the suspicions that bounce around my head like hailstones.

"Oh." My heart is beating too fast, and I nearly drop the card as I turn it over. There's blood on my fingertips, but the underside of the white card stock is unstained, so it's easy to read the name when Amanda shines her light over it.

*Jean-Guy Durand*

*Journaliste et sommelier*

"Whose is it?" Amanda asks.

"The journalist's," I say.

She makes a skeptical noise. "He's in the habit of leaving a calling card?"

It's a bit too convenient, but my desire to go to bed has evaporated.

"Where are you going?"

I've already turned toward the kitchen when Amanda grabs my wrist.

"To find him." I shake the card at her.

"And then what? Think about it. If he killed Vincent and you ask him, what's he going to do?"

I press my lips together on the childish retort that she can't tell me what to do. Still, even without saying anything, I still get a quick twist of a smile that might as well tell me I'm adorable and a good girl. I roll my eyes, and I can't help but sigh as I say, "He's going to deny it."

"If you're lucky," she says. "If you're not lucky, he'll kill you too."

The hairs on the back of my neck stand on end, and Amanda nods. "Right. The best thing for you to do is go sleep in the boathouse, and tomorrow, we'll get help."

"Is that what you're going to do?" I ask. She arches an eyebrow, and I realize what I've said. The memory of her kiss still makes my ears heat, and I'm lucky it's dark so Amanda can't see.

"I'd prefer to stay close to you to make sure you're safe." She won't quite meet my gaze as she says it, though.

I clear my throat. "What I meant to say was, what about everyone else? If it's not safe for me, what about the others?"

"No one else seems to suspect anything. The easiest thing for the killer to do is hide in plain sight until they can escape. If we don't let on that we suspect anything, we'll all get out of this safely."

On the other side of the fallen tree, a glass shatters and a woman screams, followed by a man's shouting.

"Get out of here before I kill you!"

# SIX

BY THE TIME we get to the kitchen, chaos has fully broken out. Half the candles have blown out, and a few more are burning on their sides where they've tipped over. As I swing my flashlight around, I spot Didi and Sloan cowering by the fridge. The kitchen staff are close by, armed with pot lids like shields. Bert is standing in the middle of the room, arms stretched out like he's warding off attacks from both sides, which . . . he pretty much is.

"Now, everyone, let's not be too hasty," he says.

"Hasty?" This is Chris, who is standing by the door to the back hall with another glass in his hand, clearly poised to throw it. "When she's been planning to leave with him for the last year?"

The glass goes flying toward Laurel on the other side of the kitchen island. The fury in her eyes is unmistakable, and the shadows from the candlelight make her appear extra purposeful as she bats the airborne glass away. It hits the wall and shatters to the floor. The woman's scream comes again, only it turns out it's not a woman at all. It's Jean-Guy, who is huddled behind an open cabinet door.

"What is going on?" I ask.

"He's lost his mind," Didi says, sounding close to tears.

"Lost my mind?" Chris asks . . . or really, he shouts. He's casting around for something else to throw, but one of the kitchen staff has been brave enough to sneak forward and grab the tray of wine glasses he's been using as ammunition. "I've been betrayed!"

"Come on, Chris. Stop," Laurel says, sounding more annoyed than frightened.

"You really think he can give you something I can't?" he asks. His whole face cracks with pain, and I can't say I blame him. Men are not my thing—they're way too emotional, for one—but unless he's got a ton of money, Jean-Guy is way too old for someone like Laurel. She can't be more than thirty, and he's definitely well into his sixties.

"I don't want to be squeezing my tits together behind a glass of Riesling while you tell me to smile for the camera for the rest of my life. Is that so hard to understand?"

The room gets quiet for a second as all our gazes ping-pong from Laurel to Chris to Laurel's chest and then literally anywhere else.

Chris laughs. "We agreed from the beginning you would be the face of the account."

"I didn't realize that would mean I'd never get to say anything." She thrusts a finger toward Jean-Guy, who shrinks back under the renewed attention. "He's going to give me a byline, Chris. A goddamn monthly column. And an expense account so I don't have to live on crackers and brie every single damn night."

Now Chris's humour dies. "But you like brie."

"You're so fucking cheap. You spend all our money on clothes and wine so we can look good for our followers. I want a life, Chris. A job."

He puts his palm to his cheek like she's slapped him, even though they're still across the room from one another.

"A job?" He makes the word sound poisonous. "We said . . . we agreed. No jobs. Just the two of us."

"I changed my mind." She folds her arms over her chest. "And Jean-Guy says I can start any time I want. So we're through, Chris. I'm sorry I didn't tell you sooner."

One of the kitchen staff whistles. Sloan mutters something to herself that sounds like a drawn-out "Awkward." Chris seems to realize he has an audience because even in the uneven candlelight, his face goes visibly red.

He says, "This place is a fucking joke. We only came for the Chateau Saint-Michel, and now, we won't get a chance to see it."

Jean-Guy makes a strangled sound. Bert clears his throat. He says, "How about we call it a night? Tensions are running high, and clearly the auction is . . ." He glances toward me, but then beyond my shoulder, no doubt to where Vincent is lying. "Anyway, let's all get some sleep."

"Yes." Sloan claps her hands. "We've got guest rooms set up for all of you. Let me show you where—"

"I'm not sleeping with him," Laurel says, jutting her chin toward Chris.

"You can sleep with your new boss instead," he says with a mean grin.

"Monsieur," Jean-Guy says, dabbing at his brow once more. "I assure you, my interest in Miss Laurel is purely professional, and—"

"I'm not sleeping with either of you," Laurel says. The tension in the kitchen is rising very quickly again. Reena and her team have raised their shields in anticipation of a new battle.

"But . . ." Sloan flaps her mouth open and closed a few times before she finds more words. "We only have enough beds for each of you. I mean, for the couples . . . er . . . the people who were couples when they arrived. And we need somewhere for Bert and Didi since they can't get home. The other rooms are spoken for. Unless someone wants to sleep on the couch in the living room."

"With the body?" Laurel sounds horrified.

"If anyone should sleep with the body, it should be you," Chris says to Sloan.

"Me?" She looks toward me. "What about—"

I hold up my hands and back away before I can be voluntold for corpse watch. "I'm sleeping in the boathouse."

"You weren't even invited to begin with," Sloan says through clenched teeth.

I scoff as the back of my neck prickles. "It's my house too, so—"

"I'll sleep in the boathouse too," Amanda says, bringing a moment of silence back to the room. Sloan bites off whatever retort she was working on. "I can share with Gillian. Laurel can have my room."

The prickle on my neck becomes a flush at the memory of her mouth on mine in the cellar . . . and so many other nights where we slept—or didn't sleep, as often happened—pressed together.

But what am I supposed to say? No one wants another standoff with Chris and Laurel. We're grown-ups. We'll set some much-needed ground rules and boundaries and get a few hours of sleep.

Before I can even agree, Sloan's nodding. "Sounds good. Thank you, Amanda, for being so accommodating." She doesn't glance at me again, but I'm pretty sure that was a dig in my direction.

The group starts to disperse, murmuring to themselves. Laurel and Chris are still glaring daggers at each other, and

Jean-Guy gives them all a very wide berth. Even Didi looks shaken, and Bert puts a consoling arm around her shoulder as he follows after the others.

I jump when another hand settles on my own shoulder.

"Sorry," Amanda says. "I hope it's okay if we share."

I shrug. "It's fine. I'm too exhausted to do anything tonight, anyway."

She tugs her bottom lip between her teeth, trying to hold back a grin, and it takes a few seconds for me to realize what I've said.

"Er . . . I mean . . . not that we'd be doing anything. Just sleeping. I'm too tired to do more than sleep . . . with anyone." Every syllable is making it worse, but I can't seem to stop.

Amanda's laugh is musical as she squeezes my arm. "Go ahead," she says. "Sloan showed me where I was supposed to sleep before you showed up. I have to get my overnight bag. Or you can wait here if you want?"

I shake my head. The walk by myself will give me a chance to clear my thoughts. The bed in the boathouse loft isn't big. Sometimes Dad used the loft as an office, and the bed was there mostly for nights he wrote deep into the dark hours and forgot to bring a flashlight down with him. It was never meant for guests or even for more than one person. I'll need a second to prepare myself before I have to squeeze in next to Amanda on the ancient mattress.

"I'll see you down there," I say, then shiver as she trails her fingers over my arm before she lets go.

The walk down to the boathouse is a chaotic mix of thoughts. Amanda and I broke up. That hasn't changed, and it isn't going to change even now that we're here together. A spy? How is that any better than a liar? It just means she won't have to make stuff up when she gets sent to a gala in Malta or whatever.

But also, probably more important than a love life that's been dead in the water since I walked away from her is the fact that I overreacted. Laurel and Jean-Guy didn't kill Vincent. They were talking jobs, not murder. I shake myself all over. This whole night has messed with my head, and now I'm seeing killers where there aren't any.

I scream as a dark shape steps onto the path in front of me.

"Who's that?" The voice is heavily accented and that plus the realization of how much bigger he is than me has my heart beating too fast. Laurel and Jean-Guy didn't kill Vincent, but someone did, and before I overheard the conversation in the guest room, Amanda was pretty sure the killer had to be Yuriy.

And now he's standing in front of me.

Don't panic. Don't panic.

I glance back toward the house. Were they not in the kitchen during the confrontation between Chris and Jean-Guy?

A hand settles on my shoulder, and I scream again, spinning around to face him, only to blind myself in the glare of his cell phone light. I hold up a hand to ward him off, and he makes a tsking sound.

"It's you," he says, sounding displeased. "You shouldn't be out here alone."

At least he lets the phone drop so it's not shining directly in my eyes. Little whorls of red and green dance in my vision like a sinister Christmas tree or a bad carnival ride.

"Can I walk you back to the house?" he asks. "It's very dark out. No moon. It's a bad sign."

Where is his wife? They've been attached at the hip since they arrived. She must be close by. Is she waiting behind the trees? Watching me? Does she have a gun with one of those night vision things that means she'll see me long before I ever see her? Leave it to my sister to invite some assassins to her wine weekend. I hope she's sorry when I'm gone.

A branch cracks, and another shape materializes from between the trees. Even in the dark, I can make out the lighter shades of Lana's dress.

"Who is this?" she asks. It's possibly the first time I've heard her say anything all night, and her voice reminds me of strong whisky on a cold night. Warm, but with a fierceness beneath that could hurt.

The light shines back at my face, and I squint.

"That's unnecessary, don't you think?" I ask.

They speak to each other in Russian. Or Belarusian? Is that a thing? He lowers the phone enough that I can see clearly again. They aren't quite as polished as before. His immaculate ponytail has slipped a few strands loose, and there's a dark mark on her dress near one hip, like she brushed against something dirty.

Whatever they're talking about, it's not going well. The whisky is turning to fire, and he's clearly rising to the occasion. I take a tentative step forward, and the light swings back up so I can't see anything as the two of them continue what is quickly becoming an argument. Can no one here solve their problems without shouting? Though the arguing could be a good thing. The longer they do it, the longer I stay alive.

All arguments come to an end, though, and as I'm about to make a run for the boathouse, Lana grabs me by the arm.

"Hey," I say, pulling back against what turns out to be a vicious grip. "Stop that."

"You come with us," she says.

"No. Let me go." Is this it? They're going to drag me off into the trees and hit me over the head with a branch. I know the woods on the island pretty well, though it's been a long time since I really went exploring. There are lots of places to hide. Fallen trees and outcroppings of rock. In the dark, they'd have a hard time finding me. But if I can't see where I'm going, I'd also have a hard time getting away without breaking an ankle—or worse, my neck.

They're arguing again while I dig my heels into the soft ground, but she refuses to let go. Whatever's about to happen, it's not good.

Over the humid night air, the off-key words of a song drift toward us. I hear it first and lean backward, straining to identify who it is and which way they're coming. But it only takes a second before Yuriy and Lana freeze, their discussion turning hushed before it cuts off entirely in—even if I don't speak the language, it's still pretty clear—a hissed curse. They let me go, and I tumble back, catching a foot on a rock or a tree root that sends me wheeling all the way over until I land in the dirt with a thud.

The singing is closer now, and Yuriy uses his phone light to search up the trail, which is how we see Amanda swinging toward us. She's got an uncorked wine bottle in one hand, and two glasses in the other, including one that is mostly full and spills drops of red wine all over the path as she weaves toward us. She's singing—badly—at the top of her lungs.

In short, Amanda looks royally drunk. I've never seen her like this before. Any time we were out at one of her work events, she was always perfectly in control. Drunk spies aren't as reliable as sober ones.

That's a thought for another time, though. I scramble backward, and Amanda nearly trips over me as she finally seems to notice we're there. I pat her foot, trying to get her attention, while Yuriy and Lana close ranks a few feet away.

"Hey, guys," Amanda says, voice bleary with the glow of good wine. "What's going on over here?"

# SEVEN

AMANDA'S WOBBLING EVEN while she stands still, and I really don't see how we're going to save each other if she can barely stay upright.

"Do you want some wine?" She thrusts her two glasses toward them. The half-full one slops wine over the lip, which spatters on the hem of Lana's dress. She sneers as she takes a step back, then seems to notice the dark streak along her leg and lets out the same unintelligible but all-too-clear curse she used a minute ago.

"Oh my gosh. I'm sorry. Let me help." Amanda sets the wine and glasses down beside me. For a split second, our gazes meet, and it could be the dim light, but I think she winks. Then she's stumbling forward even while she's still straightening. The effect is to have both Yuriy and Lana retreating at her approach, since she looks like she might take out one or both like a linebacker.

"Stop," Yuriy says, at the same time Lana says, "No thank you."

But Amanda will not be denied. She reaches forward, snagging Lana's skirt, then trips again, and sends them both tumbling to the ground. The whole time, she's going, "Oh gosh. Oh gosh. I'm so sorry," as she paws at the material, and Lana swears. Finally, Yuriy has to intervene. He more or less lifts Amanda off his wife and tosses her toward me. I hope she manages to avoid the pointiest of the rocks, though she still lands with a grunt.

Yuriy is helping Lana to her feet. Her lovely pink dress has turned dark with mud, and even her pale skin is streaked with it. Amanda's still apologizing even as she struggles to orient herself.

"I'm really sorry. Do you want some wine?" She holds the bottle up again, even as she basically continues to roll in the dirt.

They don't even answer. Yuriy puts an arm around Lana's waist and escorts her past us. She's yelling and swearing the whole time, but soon enough her shouts fade into the trees as they head toward the house.

On the ground beside me, Amanda laughs. I'm holding my breath and let it out in a rush as I shove at her.

"What the hell?" I ask.

She snorts and smothers a laugh by taking a swig directly from the bottle. I fumble for my phone and swing the light in her direction. She's propped up on one elbow, and her gaze on me is totally clear. In the blue beam of light, she spins the bottle to examine the label.

"Chateau Deveaux-Gauthier. 1977. Not bad. A hint of leather and barnyard. Just the way I like it."

I roll my eyes. "You're totally sober, aren't you?"

"Of course. How long has it been? Five minutes? Even if I downed the whole bottle, it wouldn't have hit me yet."

"Is that something they teach you in spy school?" I climb to my feet and hold a hand out to her. I mean to help her up, but she passes me the wine glasses instead and gets up on her own, brushing the dirt from her clothes as she goes.

"There's no such thing as spy school, Gilly," she says with a grin. "I have an MBA from Western, remember?"

"Huh, at least that part is true," I mutter to myself. There's a new flash of something in Amanda's eyes at that, but I turn away before she can say anything else. I expect her to follow, but there's only the sound of steps crunching on pine needles heading away from me. I turn, swinging the light. Amanda's halfway up the path.

"Where are you going?" I call. After my run-in with Muskoka's visiting crime couple, I don't want to be out here alone anymore.

"I left my bag behind a tree." She's at the limit of what my phone can illuminate, and as she speaks, she disappears off the path, only to reappear a second later with a leather tote I recognize. It's her I'll-only-be-gone-one-night bag. The sight of it by the door always made my heart drop. Now she swings it with her free hand. "It didn't fit with my party girl cover story." She's still smiling, but all I can do is wonder how many other cover stories there have been. This whole night has messed with my head in the worst ways.

"What did they want?" Amanda asks as we head toward the water.

"I'm not sure. He sort of showed up in front of me while I was headed to the boathouse. He asked what I was doing and said it wasn't safe to be out here alone. Then he grabbed me, but you showed up before anything could happen."

Amanda laughs. "Spooky."

We're quiet for a while. Water laps at the dock as we reach the boathouse.

"Do you think they killed Vincent?"

"Someone did. And based on that domestic up there, I don't think it was the wine kids or the journalist."

"Kids?" I scoff. "They're not much younger than I am."

"Anyone who thinks influencer is a real job will always be a child in my books."

"As opposed to pretending to be a banker? Most of us grow out of make-believe by the time we hit middle school."

Oops. That was the thing I was trying not to say.

Amanda's ahead of me, and she doesn't reply as she opens the door to the boathouse. Inside is as dark as out, and I hesitate at the threshold. Who knows what's lurking in there?

"Come on." She cocks her head. "You need some sleep. Tonight's been a lot." When I continue to pause, she says, "Just sleep, I promise."

Her consideration is enough to get me moving again. I take a long drink of the wine. It does taste like barnyard, but I'm not in the mood to debate whether or not that's a bad thing. I push past her and into the boathouse, taking another swig for fortification.

"Don't want to use the glasses?" Amanda asks as she climbs the stairs behind me.

"You'll kiss me, but you won't share a bottle of wine?"

She laughs. "Sorry about that. I had to think on the fly."

"Another one of those spy school tricks?"

She doesn't answer. Instead, she walks around the space with the same comfort she used to navigate the house. She knows the loft as well as I do. We snuck down here on more than one night. Making out like teenagers when the family togetherness got to be too much. Amanda was my refuge as much as the boathouse was.

She finds an old gas camping lantern and lights it with some waterproof matches. It's the first stable light I've seen in hours, and I have to squint for a second. Amanda takes the bottle from my grip and pours what's left in it into the glasses. She holds one out to me, and I gulp it down faster than is probably socially acceptable. If it's any comfort, Amanda does the same, and when we're done treating a rare vintage wine like it's tequila shots, we stare at each other, breathless.

Amanda says, "Another one?"

I swish the bottle. "None left."

She taps her brow and rummages in the overnight bag before producing a fresh bottle. This one isn't from Dad's collection. I've seen the label at the store. One of those weird Australian brands with a name like Goats in the Bush.

"You brought that yourself?" I ask.

"I'm not much for that fussy French stuff."

"Then why are you even here?"

The question comes out harsher than I mean it to. But Amanda nods, so she must have been expecting it. She pours us each a glass.

"The organization I worked for likes to have a toehold in events like this. They're prime opportunities for money laundering, so if we can put someone in the room, it gives us a better chance to monitor the guests. In this case, it was easy enough to get an invite from Bert." Her gaze at me is guilty. "If I'd known you were going to be here, I might have asked them to send someone else."

That's not much of a comfort. Also, it may be an answer to my question, but it breeds a hundred more.

"And who exactly do you work for?"

She shrugs, like we're talking about a new movie or the weather forecast. "I worked in wealth management for eight years. You remember. Lots of high-profile clients with assets around the world. And after a while, I started to notice some things."

"What kind of things?"

"Irregularities. Around the office. Not with the clients. Invites to events for charities that didn't exist when I looked online. Art bought at auctions, then the same art would disappear from the office walls a week later."

I whistle. "Who buys office art at auction? I worked for an agency that bought it on Amazon."

"You do if you're laundering money under the table for clients."

Too bad I already used up my whistle. I settle for a sip of wine. "Sounds sneaky."

"I raised it with the higher-ups and figured that was it. But it kept happening. So then I went to the authorities. Turned out it was happening in a couple of offices. Millions of dollars coming from Eastern Europe and going back all squeaky clean."

In my head, money laundering involves stacks of dollar bills tumbling around in a spin cycle. But I'm pretty sure that's not what she means.

"So how do you go from that to secret identities and cover stories?"

She smiles. For the first time, the expression is relaxed. "I keep telling you it's not like that. There's no secret identity. If anyone looks me up, I'm Amanda Mulgrave, senior partner at Cougar Capital Partners."

I bite back the obvious cougar joke. We're not that old yet. But she laughs anyway. "I got a call. After the dust settled on the laundering thing."

"They made you an offer you couldn't refuse?" Now I'm smiling too, and the expression grows as she laughs harder.

"That's the mob. This was the CRA."

Okay, that's the funniest thing she's said yet. "The Canada Revenue Agency? Like the guys who tell me I screwed up on my taxes?"

"They do more than that. There's a task force that investigates suspected money laundering. The CRA, RCMP, FINSTAR. They're all involved. But they need people like me with contacts in the industry. The CRA guys know their stuff, but like you said, they're not exactly the life of the party."

I toast her with my glass. "You can certainly play the part. Remember that guy with the suspenders and the supermodel girlfriend at the gala in Montreal? He talked your ear off for an hour about international stock exchanges."

She grins. "That supermodel was a French assassin."

I nearly drop my wine. Red droplets splatter on the sheets. "What?"

"Just kidding. She was just a model."

"Very funny." I roll my eyes and take a fresh sip. No barnyard this time. Just some cherries and those raisins in tiny boxes from preschool snack time.

"Suspenders was an art forger, though. A good one too."

"What? He was old enough to be my grandfather. His hands shook when he tried to drink from a glass."

She shrugs. "That was also a cover. Who would believe an aging man with tremors was responsible for one of the biggest art scams of the last fifty years?"

And my mind is a blur again. Seems to be the speed tonight is going to go at.

"What happened to him?" If he was arrested, Amanda wasn't involved. We finished that party stumbling drunk down Sainte-Catherine Street and eating poutine in our evening gowns.

"He's still at it. There are rumors about a fake Vermeer found in a collection that had been loaned to the Louvre. They said it was so accurate, right down to the brush strokes, the only way they were able to prove it wasn't original was by carbon dating the wood the canvas was mounted on."

"So who cares, then? If even the experts can't tell, what does it matter who painted it?" After everything, it's nice to sit and have a conversation with someone. There's no sound down here but the gentle wash of water in the boat slip, and the glow of the lantern barely reaches the corners of the loft. We might as well be a million miles away from the chaos and damage of the house.

"It's a long game. In another decade or so, someone will find the genuine article"—she uses air quotes around "find"—"and the lore of it being lost will drive up the price. If you're looking to launder money but don't mind waiting to move your cash, it's pretty effective. Art auctions are more heavily regulated now, so it's harder to inflate prices through anonymous bidders and things like that. The people in that world have gotten more creative."

The way she says "that world" makes it sound like something else. The kind of place you read about in a book. But she's part of it, isn't she? Even if she's on the good guys' side, she lives in a completely different sphere than the one I believed she did. Than the one I still live in today.

"Were you ever going to tell me?"

I don't mean to ask, but oh, look. My wine glass is empty. Six years ago, I wanted answers, and tonight, I'm going to get them.

Amanda at least has the good grace to twist her lips in a grimace. "There are rules about that kind of thing. NDAs. I work with this guy who's been married to his husband for seven years and still tells him he works for a call centre."

"That's super shitty," I say, pouring more wine. She acknowledges the comment with a silent toast.

"It's not the way I'd do it now, but . . ." She swishes a mouthful around as she thinks.

"But it's the way you did it then," I finish the thought for her. She nods as she finishes her glass and pours another.

"I'm sorry," she says. "I've been sorry for a long time."

That's nice of her to say. Not that she didn't apologize back then. We're Canadian, after all. When I pushed her to come clean, she said she was sorry over and over. But she never told the truth. And now that she has, I don't know that we could have done any differently back then. A spy? It doesn't sound like she's jumping out of planes or engaging in high-speed motorcycle chases around the narrow streets of some ancient European city. But what would I do when we both get back from our respective jobs, I ask how her day was, and she says that information is classified? I asked for honesty, and she's given it to me, but it turns out it's not enough.

By the time I finish my second glass, my head is swimming. Emotional turmoil makes me a lightweight. I flop down on the bed, staring up at the rafters that are half hidden in shadow. A second later, Amanda lies down next to me, also facing up. In the double bed, we're touching even without trying. Her shoulder brushes against mine, and I close my eyes.

"There's one thing I'm not sorry about," she says.

"What's that?" I smile, enjoying the warmth of the wine in my veins.

"Kissing you. Before. I lied when I apologized. I'm sorry for lying, but I don't regret kissing you."

The admission tightens a lump in my chest. I rub at my sternum, trying to loosen it, but the motion makes it worse.

She shifts, and when she speaks again, her breath puffs against my cheek.

"I really missed you, Gilly."

We'll blame the wine for the tear that escapes from the corner of my eye. I roll over to hide it. Beside me, Amanda sighs, but she doesn't touch me again. We lie in silence for a while. Finally, she says, "I am sorry about your dad, though. That sucks."

Ah, yeah. Now I'm crying for real.

"Thanks."

"I thought about going to the funeral, but I wasn't sure if showing up would piss you off."

Would it have? I can't even say anymore.

"He always liked you," I say. "He was mad when I broke up

with you. Said I should give you another chance." I was so mad right back at him. How dare he take Amanda's side over mine?

"No, you were right." Now she puts a hand on my shoulder, rolling me over again so I'm facing her. Without meaning to, I snuggle in, and she wraps her arms around me. Her cheek is on my hair and the smell of her—sandalwood and amber, familiar and comforting—is in my nose. "If you can't be honest with the person you care about most in the world, what kind of life is that?"

My heart swells with a dozen different emotions. I've missed her so much. That's the honest truth of it. There were so many days I thought of something silly to text her and then realized I'd deleted her number. So many nights I thought about finding someone on an app who was looking for a quick hookup, to take the edge off, only to realize it wouldn't be enough. All I'd wanted was Amanda to hold me like this and tell me everything was going to be okay.

"I really miss my dad." My voice cracks.

She squeezes me tighter. "Gilly." My name is a soft breath on her lips, and I chase it until my mouth finds hers. I'm such a mess. This whole night is. But it doesn't matter. Tonight could be all there is, and if that's true, I'm not wasting any more of it.

I twine my fingers in her hair and pull just enough so she knows what I want. She stills, and I keep kissing her, sucking in the smell and taste of her with all my senses. Finally, she relaxes. Her hands move from my back to my hips. She kisses my cheeks, blotting out the tears there. It doesn't take me much work to pull her shirt free of her linen trousers, and I groan when I find the warm, breathing flesh underneath.

"Touch me," I say. "Please." If she doesn't touch me soon, I might explode.

"Gilly," she says, rolling me onto my back and pinning me down.

"Please. Please, I need it. Need you." My whole body rolls with heat and want. Whatever we have tonight, I won't regret it, even if I never see her again.

Outside, a woman screams.

"Oh my god, I think he's dead!"

# EIGHT

I'LL BE HONEST: my sister is the queen of coitus interruptus. It started the summer I turned eighteen when she found me in this very same boathouse. I had Brianna Tilberg's head between my thighs, and Sloan walked in. She swore she was looking for a life jacket, but we never kept those in the loft. That was the first time, but it wasn't the last. Most recently, she found Amanda and me in the coat closet at one of Bert and Didi's annual Christmas parties in Toronto. I had my hand up Amanda's skirt and was not prepared for my sister's "What the fuck are you doing?" I was, however, very ready to become an only child in that moment.

But this may take the cake. I'm still coming back to earth, hormones racing, but Amanda's already on her feet and rushing toward the stairs. She grabs the lantern as she goes by, so my only option is to follow her if I don't want to get left in the dark. My shirt is untucked and the top button is undone, but fortunately—and so, *so* unfortunately—I don't need any light to get myself put back together and rush outside.

Among the dark trees, the screaming has stopped, but the sound of a woman weeping flows toward us, followed by other voices calling out questions. Lights appear overhead as people come out to the deck.

"What's going on?" someone asks.

"Sloan? Sweetie, what happened?" That's Didi.

We find Sloan sitting on the ground, arms wrapped around her knees. Her crying has evolved to heaving sobs that shake her whole body. Her phone is lying in the dirt, casting an eerie blueish light around her. When she looks up at me, her face is streaked with dirt and tears, and her immaculate hair is sticking out in wild clumps like she's been pulling at it.

A man lies next to her. It's Jean-Guy. His arms and legs are at weird angles. Amanda lifts the lantern, making the shadows shift, and for a second, I think his open eyes stare right at me, and I scream. But then, as the light settles, I realize his head is twisted farther than a head should, and he's not blinking or looking at anything in particular.

"Is he dead?" Laurel asks from the deck. I can't see them as their little flashlights shine down on us, but there are four beams of light.

"Careful," Didi says. "The rail is broken."

I reach forward, brushing my hand over Jean-Guy's face. His eyelids slide shut, and his skin is still warm under my fingertips. I'm still expecting him to come to. Shake his head and ask me what I'm doing.

"No." Sloan shakes her head as she scrabbles onto her hands and knees. She reaches for Jean-Guy, shaking him. "He's not dead. He can't be dead. No, please." The tears return, and she wails loudly. Finally, she slumps against him, head pressed to his chest as she cries. It's a pathetic scene by any definition, and I can't help myself as I gently take hold of her and pull her to me, stepping away from the corpse. She's weeping like she's lost a loved one. Like I did when Dad died, and I don't understand.

"It's okay," I say, smoothing out her hair.

"Did anyone see what happened?" Amanda asks the people watching overhead.

"I think he fell?" Laurel says.

"Yes, but did you actually see it? Did he fall or did someone push him over? Was he out here with anyone else?"

With every question, Sloan sobs harder and harder against me. I walk us away, so the conversation fades.

"It's okay," I say again. "Sloan. Take a breath. Everything will be okay."

"It won't," she moans. "I've made a mess of everything. What am I going to do now?"

"What do you mean you've made a mess?" My heart stutters in my chest at the fleeting thought my sister might be a murderer. But that's impossible. We have our differences, and the last few months have been awful, but she wouldn't go this far. She's spoiled and selfish, but she's not capable of killing someone.

She sniffles, rubbing her nose against my shirt, and I grimace. Part of me was still hoping we'd get whatever happened here cleared up, and Amanda and I could go back to the boathouse. But I can't expect her to make out with me if there's snot on my clothes.

"I'm never going to sell this place now," Sloan says, still clinging to me. "No one's going to want to buy a house where two people died. Do you think we can just not tell them?"

There goes any kind-hearted feelings I was starting to have toward my sister. I push her off me, then trip over a root for my trouble, barely managing to catch myself on a sticky pine tree.

"That's all you think about, isn't it?" I scoff. "I can't believe you. What happened to us sharing responsibility? We agreed, Sloan."

It's too dark to see more than a shadow, but I think she rubs her nose with the back of her hand. Better than my shirt. Her tone could curdle milk as she says, "And what were you going to do with it, Gilly? You haven't even come up here once since Dad died. It's just sitting here. Bruno and I . . . It hasn't been a good year for him, okay? The market . . . the corporate clients aren't buying, and the collectors have moved on to some new artistic wunderkind in Vancouver who paints with fire extinguishers. I thought . . ." She sighs, slapping her hands against her thighs like she's trying to clean them. "You know what? Never mind. Doesn't matter now. The house is ruined. We don't have the money to fix it up, and no one will buy it when they find out people died here."

"There's insurance," I say. "The tree. Stuff like that happens up here all the time."

"No, there isn't," she says.

"There isn't what?"

"Insurance. The house isn't insured."

"What? Why not?"

"Forget it." She goes to walk past me, and I grab her wrist.

"No, I'm not going to forget it. What do you mean it's not insured?"

She whirls, and this close I can see the flash of anger in her eyes. "Because I stopped paying it, okay? A couple of months ago."

I rock on my heels, clinging to the tree even harder than before.

"You stopped paying it? What made you think that was a good idea?" You can't not insure places up here. They can sit empty for months at a time. Trees fall, waterfronts flood. There was a wildfire not far from here a few years ago. Hell, a family nearby had a bear that decided their cottage would be a perfect den for hibernation and spent a winter slowly taking the place apart from the inside in an effort to find the right spot for his long nap. Acts of nature are inevitable in these parts.

"It was expensive." She's whining.

"Of course it's expensive. It's a house on an island miles from the nearest fire hydrant. That's all the more reason to have insurance."

"Stop yelling at me!" I don't need light to picture the way her bottom lip is sticking out or the way she stamps her foot. "We've never needed it before. And Bruno and I needed the money. He said—"

"Bruno said? You chose Bruno over this place? How could you be so careless?"

"What was I supposed to do? You weren't talking to me. Dad's gone. I did the best I could, Gilly."

"Your best sucks." I spin and stalk away from my sister before I add another body to the pile. In typical fashion, she follows after me, still whining like a scolded child.

The lantern is still on the ground by Jean-Guy. Someone has found another turtle towel and laid it over him, though his arms and legs stick out from under it. Muffled voices come from overhead, so I pick up the lantern and make my way back up the staircase to the house. The candles are lit in the kitchen once again, and they're all gathered around the island, though everyone has given space to the people they didn't come with. Chris and Laurel appear to have made up now that Laurel's job prospects are on shaky ground. Didi and Bert are near the fridge. Yuriy and Lana are near the door to the dining room, and they give me a cold stare as I enter. I shrink back instinctively, and Sloan bumps into my back, protesting my carelessness.

"What about them? Where were you?" Chris points an accusatory finger at me—or possibly Sloan—and everyone else's attention swings our way. I step to the side, having no desire to be associated with my sister once again.

"We were talking," I say, glancing at Amanda. Her lips are pinched tight, and her face is serious.

"Not now. Before that. What were you doing before he died?"

Oh, for fuck's sake. Everything about this night pisses me off, from Sloan's incompetence to the smug expression on Chris's face.

"I was with Amanda," I say. I'm not shy. If they need to be told I was kissing my ex and wanting things I can't have, I'll tell them.

"And you?" Chris says, clearly still fishing for suspects.

"I was . . ." Sloan wraps her arms around herself protectively. "I was going for a walk."

"In the dark?" He laughs. I want to slap him for being an asshole.

"Are you accusing my sister of something?" I may be mad at her, but no one gets to talk shit about Sloan except me.

"Who goes for a walk in the dark on a murder island?" he says.

"If anyone was going to kill him, it would be you," I say. "He was trying to steal your girl."

"No one was stealing me." Laurel sounds indignant that I would even suggest it, and I feel bad for a split second. In the choice between Chris the jerk and Jean-Guy, I can't say which I'd actually pick . . . other than the fact one is dead now. Even so, I might still choose a corpse over Chris.

"I didn't kill anyone!" Sloan starts to cry again. A whole chorus of accusations and protests goes up around her. Didi's hugging Sloan, and Bert is asking for cooler heads to prevail. Chris clearly disagrees and seems to be yelling at everyone all at once, while Laurel shouts at him to stop. Even Yuriy and Lana get drawn into the fray as Chris turns his suspicions toward them. Yuriy steps protectively in front of Lana and stomps toward Chris with murder in his eyes—regardless of who else he may or may not have killed tonight. Amanda spots Chris's doom before he does and puts herself between them, raising her hands and her voice over the chaos.

"Okay." The word careens off the walls. "That's enough from everyone."

The shouting dies, though Yuriy still looks like he wants to pull Chris's fingernails out one at a time. Sloan's whimpering. Somewhere along the way, the cooks and kitchen staff have appeared to see what the commotion is. They all look scared, and for the first time, I finally realize what's going on here. People are dead. Someone has killed them both. And that someone is standing in this room. And sure, I guess I understood that before, but I was so caught up in Sloan's shittiness and Amanda's sudden reappearance in my life with all her fun revelations that I didn't have a chance to get scared.

I'm officially scared now.

Chris and Yuriy take a step back, though neither of them looks away. One's a known criminal, the other clearly has a temper—and a motive. Laurel's pulling at him, and he's still got his caveman face on.

I slide my hand into Amanda's. For once, my words all catch in my throat. I glance from Yuriy to Chris, then do a general swivel of the whole room. She swallows and nods before she leads me to where Sloan and Didi are standing. They aren't exactly the picture of comfort. I'd rather stay with Amanda, but she gives me a gentle shove, and my back collides with the kitchen cabinets. She nods one more time, then turns and lets her voice carry over the space.

"Okay, everyone. Listen. This is a murder investigation, and I'm in charge. No more accusations. We're doing this my way from now on."

It's time for Amanda, the spy.

# NINE

TURNS out not everyone buys into Amanda's authority as quickly as I'd like.

"But you're a wealth manager," Bert says, looking mystified.

"We really should wait for the police," Didi agrees.

"Who said for sure either of them was killed?" Laurel asks. "What if it was an accident?"

"Both of them?" Reena, the chef asks, and Laurel shrugs.

"The railing is broken," Bert says. "It could have given way, and Jean-Guy fell?"

Didi gasps. "But if he fell, wouldn't he have called out for help?"

"That's what we need to figure out," Amanda says.

"Are you sure you didn't do it?" Chris asks. "You could be taking charge here so no one suspects you." He smiles like he's the smartest guy in the room.

Amanda sighs. "Because I was busy."

My cheeks heat, followed by my ears. No one's even watching me, but they might as well all be staring.

"Doing what?" He's still smirking. How does Laurel not punch him on a daily basis?

"She was with me," I say quickly. "We were in the boathouse. Yuriy and Lana saw us on our way down."

The two of them scowl, clearly displeased to be drawn into this. They have a silent conversation made up mostly of pursed lips and Lana's painted fingernails tapping on her wrist, but finally, Yuriy gives a tight nod.

"We did."

He also—assuming he's paying attention, and I have to assume he is—saw Amanda behaving like she was falling down drunk, and now she is clearly very sober. She hasn't actually told the others what she does for a living, and the reason for that is undoubtedly Yuriy and Lana's presence. If they know what she is, they also know the kinds of people Amanda would prefer that information not reach.

"Didi saw us earlier too," I rush on to say. If Amanda can't tell the whole truth, it's like I have to fill in as many blanks as I can without giving too much away. "We were . . ." I clear my throat. "We were kissing in the wine cellar."

"It's true. I did see them," Didi says eagerly, like she's relieved to have something to contribute. "Oh, Gilly, I'm so happy for you. The two of you were always so—"

"Then what about your walk?" Chris asks Sloan, clearly disinterested in my love life.

"What about you?" Amanda asks him before Sloan can answer. "Where were you for the last half hour?"

"I was with Laurel." He reaches for her, but she twists her hand away from him and wrinkles her nose.

"Not like that. He came to my room to ask for another chance. We were talking."

"The whole time?" Amanda asks.

She shakes her head. "It was a short conversation. Ten minutes?"

"Laurel," Chris says through gritted teeth. "You don't think I killed him, do you?"

"No one's accusing anyone of anything," Amanda says, though now she's speaking to the whole room. "We need a sense of the sequence of events."

"But he's the one who had a reason to kill him," Reena says. "What do the rest of us have to do with any of this? I never spoke to either of them."

"I didn't kill anyone!" Chris slaps his palm on the granite counter so hard glasses in the cabinet behind me rattle.

"Okay," Amanda says. "That's enough. You," she points at Chris. "Sit. Everyone else, find a seat too."

"Who put you in charge?" He pouts.

She sighs and fishes into her pocket. Amanda pulls out a billfold, which she flips open to show an official-looking badge and a greenish-looking picture of herself staring seriously back at the camera.

"Because I work for a Canadian task force on domestic terrorism, and I'm the closest thing we have to police until the actual police arrive."

The silent room gets even quieter. Everyone stares at Amanda. She doesn't stay anything further as she slides the ID back into her pocket. There's some grumbling, but Chris flings himself onto a chair. The rest follow shortly. When the chairs are gone, the kitchen staff hops up on the counters. Chris looks like he might try to pull Laurel into his lap, but she steps away and leans against the window. Yuriy and Lana choose to remain where they are.

"Now," Amanda says, "one at a time. I was with Gillian in the boathouse."

When she glances at me, I say, "I was with you in the boathouse."

It's like the most sinister icebreaker ever. Hello, my name is Gillian, and here's what I was doing when a man was killed.

"Bert and I were in bed," Didi says.

Bert nods. "It's true, we were. Didi was listening to her meditation app."

She smiles softly. "It has Bruce Leslie. Do you remember him from that hospital TV show? His voice is so soothing. I listen to him every night. Puts me to sleep right away."

Chris makes an irritated noise. Yuriy looks like he might actually be trying to smother a laugh, which has me also biting down on a giggle, partly because I'm getting punchy from stress and lack of sleep and partly because I didn't even think he could laugh in the first place.

Sloan sighs heavily and says, "I was going for a walk."

"Did anyone see you?" Chris asks. She shakes her head and won't meet anyone's gaze. Didi gives her a reassuring squeeze.

Next is the kitchen staff. Reena speaks for them. "We were downstairs in the games room."

"All of you?" Amanda asks, and there's a general nod. I grimace. The games room has a pool table and a selection of ancient couches that were carried out here on various boat trips over the years. There would have been a place for each of them to crash tonight, but it wouldn't have been the most comfortable night's sleep for anyone.

There's an awkward pause when she reaches Yuriy and Lana. For a second, it looks like they might not say anything at all, before Yuriy says, "We were in bed."

"You were down on the path," I say without meaning to, and the glance he shoots me is enough to make my knees wobble.

"And then we went to bed," Lana says, her voice flat. She's practically daring someone to argue with her, so of course Chris has to open his mouth and say, "One of you is lying."

"Chris," Laurel hisses at him, clearly aware of the threat he still hasn't spotted.

"Someone killed him, and it wasn't you or me, so one of them is lying because we're the only people here."

The mood is turning again. Everyone is tired. Probably scared too. No one wants to be accused of being a murderer or admit they're sharing a house with one.

Amanda asks, "And what were you both doing?"

"I told you I was with Laurel," Chris says.

"For ten minutes," Sloan says.

Amanda puts a hand up, asking for calm. "Where did you go after you left Laurel's room?"

"Back to my room," he says.

"And you stayed in your room?" Amanda asks Laurel.

She nods, then frowns. "I went to brush my teeth, but the water wasn't working. I saw him in the hallway." She points at Yuriy. He once again looks unhappy to be associated with any of us, but finally, he nods confirmation.

We all assess what we've learned. Strictly speaking, it's not good news for Sloan and Chris, though I don't think we can rule out Yuriy and Lana, what with the skulking around in the dark and being all menacing when I was trying to get to the boathouse.

"Okay. Everyone stay here," Amanda says. "No one leaves this room until I come back. You'll be safest together."

As she walks out of the kitchen toward the back hallway, the others are tense. Once she's out of easy earshot, there are going to be a million questions at once, and I don't want to answer any of them.

But the very second she disappears into the dark, she pokes her head back through the doorway. It's so sudden Chris clacks his jaw shut, no doubt choking back his next round of accusations. She holds up the lantern so I can clearly see she's looking directly at me.

"Are you coming?"

I feel like I've been called down to the principal's office as I duck past Sloan. There must be several pairs of eyes boring holes in my back, but I don't acknowledge any of them as I follow after Amanda. She reaches behind her, and I grab her hand. It's too narrow to walk side by side, but touching her helps ground me. Behind us, voices filter from the kitchen, though at least the yelling has stopped for now.

"Are you okay?" I whisper.

"Of course. Why wouldn't I be?"

"Because you . . ." I struggle to come up with the term. "Blew your cover, or whatever."

She snorts softly. "There's no joint Canadian task force on domestic terrorism."

"What?"

"Or there probably is, but I'm not part of it."

"But the badge," I say, still trying to understand.

"A fake. I try not to use it. But if I say financial crimes, people start bitching about mortgage rates. Domestic terrorism shuts them up in an emergency, and Chris was definitely trying to make this an emergency."

"If we do nothing else, we need to make sure Laurel dumps his ass."

She squeezes my hand. "Pretty sure she's figured that part out on her own."

We're in one of the guest rooms. It's pristine. Old brass bed frame. Rustic dresser. Tall closet. I don't need to open it to remember exactly what the inside smells like, stuffed with decades of blankets that rarely get used.

The only things out of place are a small suitcase and a matching shoulder bag. They're both made of brown leather.

The suitcase lies on the bed and is unopened. The bag is on the dresser and the straps on the top have been unbuckled. A laptop pokes out through the opening.

"Check the suitcase," Amanda says.

"For what?" I ask as I unzip it. The leather is soft under my fingertips, and the zipper is strong but undoes like a knife through butter. Jean-Guy's luggage is expensive.

"Anything that tells us who might have had a reason to kill him."

"Like the bloody business card next to Vincent's body means Jean-Guy might have killed him?"

"We need a motive," she says as she powers up the laptop. "It's possible someone killed Jean-Guy in retaliation for Vincent."

"Or else it's the same person who killed them both?" The inside of the suitcase is underwhelming. He is—or was—a boxers guy. Two button-down shirts, another pressed pair of pants. His socks might be made of silk; they're so slippery between my fingers. His shaving kit includes small bottles of unscented shampoo and hand lotion. His toothpaste is a brand I don't recognize that proudly proclaims it is "flavour-free."

"Or someone who was in on it with Jean-Guy and is trying to cover their tracks."

"Like Laurel?" I frown at the toothpaste. "Who doesn't want to be minty fresh?"

Amanda takes the tube from me, squeezes a bit of white paste onto a finger, and scrubs it against her teeth. She wrinkles her nose and spits on the floor.

"That's disgusting. But it's probably so it doesn't change the flavour of wines he's tasting. Laurel's not a killer. Yuriy might have been using him for something. If that's the case, we'll probably never find out, but at least if we keep everyone together for the rest of the night, they're less likely to hurt anyone else."

"Unless they kill us all," I grumble as I dump the suitcase out entirely and check the insides for hidden pockets. I still don't really understand what I'm looking for. A gun? A signed letter from the killer saying they're sorry but Jean-Guy deserved it?

Nothing.

"Check this," Amanda says, tossing a notebook toward me. It's bound in a leather cover that's the same brown as the rest of Jean-Guy's luggage. She hardly even looks at me, tapping through screens on the laptop.

"Didn't he have a password?" I ask.

"One, two, three, four, five," she says. "Doesn't matter what language you speak, half the world uses that as the password on their most important data."

My girlfriend is the most kickass spy ever.

I freeze at the thought. She's not my girlfriend. I can't go there. It's nice to see her again. To talk. Touch. But even with the truth between us now, it's still not the whole truth, so there isn't a future for us. Not if she's spending her days stealing secrets and rubbing elbows with criminals. I have a nice life in Toronto. A quiet one. I have a good job. A nice condo. I can't be lying awake at night wondering where she is and if she'll come back.

The notebook is full of lists and dates. Or years, I guess. Vintages. It's all in French, though, so I'm not much help.

Amanda, of course, is fluent. I always admired the way she could switch between languages. We went to a gala one night where she spent the entire evening laughing with an MP from Chicoutimi and a businessman from Martinique. I had no idea what they were saying. And now that I'm thinking about it, I can't help but wonder what her angle was. Money laundering. That's what she said, right? Did she think the businessman was bribing the MP? Buying contracts?

Is this how it's going to be? Whether I ever see Amanda again or not, am I going to spend the rest of my life going back through every night, every event? Will I be second-guessing her motivations constantly? The unfairness of it while she goes off and lives her life knowing the answers to everything tastes sour in the back of my throat.

And Amanda, of course, knows none of this. She's pinching her bottom lip between two fingers as she clicks through screens. Her eyebrows pinch together in the centre.

"See anything?" I ask.

She wrinkles her nose. "A winery called Domaine Saint-Arnault?" She points at a list of wines. "Do you recognize any of these? Does your dad have any of them?"

"I couldn't say." There are so many things I ultimately didn't know about my dad either, from his favourite kind of wine to the ticking time bomb in his chest, otherwise known as a blocked artery. But as I watch her scroll through the screen, recognition strikes me, and she pauses when I put a hand on her shoulder.

"Wait," I say, pointing at the label in Jean-Guy's document. It looks familiar. Domaine Saint-Arnault. Grand Cru. 1965. The logo depicts a stately home facing a lake and bordered by ancient trees.

"What about it?" she asks.

"I think I *have* seen that name."

"In the cellar?"

"Maybe? Does it mean anything?"

She starts scrolling again. "Hard to say right away. Jean-Guy was certainly interested in the vineyard. There's an entire history and dates when different wines were sold at auctions." Amanda whistles low. "Expensive. This one from 1947 sold for almost a hundred thousand dollars."

And my dad owned one of these? Would that be worth killing someone over? Except Dad's already dead.

"Let's go check," I say, picking up the lantern.

She follows after me as we make our way through the house. The kitchen is quiet. Reena's got the gas stove going, and the air smells like garlic and butter. If you can't accuse them all of being murderers, the next best option is to feed them, I guess. There are a few silent glances as we pass through toward the dining room, but everyone is either too tired or too busy chewing to say anything.

We go down to the cellar. The bottles reflect little starbursts of light from the lantern. Carefully, we make our way around the racks, picking through the bottles. It's tricky. French people may make excellent wine, but they don't go out of their way to make the labels easily distinguishable. Everyone uses the same book print fonts and the same stuffy images of curling grapevines or manor homes older than my country.

Finally, though, we find Domaine Saint-Arnault.

"Here," I say, waving Amanda over. She takes the lantern from me and holds it overhead as I pull out five bottles. All Domaine Saint-Arnault. All Grand Cru. 1965. The tags with Dad's notes on them dangle from each bottle neck. On the nearest shelves, the bottles are from other vineyards and much newer. The closest in date is 1997. "How much do you think these are worth?"

Amanda shrugs. "This is when a cell signal would be really handy."

"This could be half a million dollars in wine." How long ago did Dad buy these? Did he understand what they were worth? Or did he buy them at some duty-free in Paris on his way home from a business trip and forget they were down here?

"But why would someone kill Jean-Guy for it?" Amanda asks. "Or Vincent, for that matter? Now the auction is canceled, and we're all stuck here. They'd be better off stealing it and finding a way off the island before anyone noticed."

I blink at the five bottles sitting motionless on the top shelf, hoping they'll reveal some secrets. But they're frozen in time. Slowly aging until they could fund a starter home—well, a starter home outside Toronto, at least—or dig whole families out of debt. They've got nothing to tell us, and we're no further ahead than we were when we went to Jean-Guy's room.

"We ask if the others know anything about the winery?" I ask.

Amanda's clearly doing the same thing, engaged in a staring contest with five bottles of wine who don't care that she exists. Finally, she shakes her head. "Let's go check Vincent's room."

We make our way upstairs. Conversation still filters from the direction of the kitchen, though I can't see anyone through the bulk of the pine tree still consuming most of the dining room. What a night. The hours before daylight are endless, and it's only a matter of time before someone decides they don't want to play by Amanda's rules after all.

I shine the lantern in the direction of Vincent's body, lying still under the turtle towel. Sloan said she'd never sell this place now, but I can't imagine how it will ever be the same again. I shine the light in different directions, taking in the features I know so well. The notches in the wood, the shelf of biographies that were Dad's preferred reading material.

The dried blood trail on the floor. Guess that part's different. Whatever happened, Vincent crawled a good fifteen feet before he collapsed.

As the light swings around the room, a flicker catches my eye beneath one of the leather wing-backed chairs. I set the lantern down and drop to my hands and knees. It's hard to position myself so I can see under the chair without blocking the light.

"What are you doing?" Amanda asks.

"One sec." My fingers connect with the cool smoothness of glass, then I hiss when one of my fingers snags on a cracked edge. I grimace as I pull it out. Without meaning to, my newly bleeding finger slides over the label on the portion of a broken bottle that must have rolled under here. I do my best to rub it away before it stains the white paper, but even with the mark, what's printed beneath is clear. A stately home, with trees on either side.

*Domaine Saint-Arnault.*

"Amanda," I say, kneeling by it. It's the same. Grand Cru. 1966.

No. Wait. That's not right.

"1966?" Amanda says.

"It was 1965 downstairs, right?"

"Yes. The year *Dr. Zhivago* was published."

I glance at her. "What does that have to do with anything?"

"It was used as propaganda by the CIA and—" She chuckles softly to herself. "Never mind. It's how I remembered the date."

"But they're all Domaine Saint-Arnault," I say. "Even if the years are different. It's the same place as in Jean-Guy's notes. That can't be a coincidence, right?"

Laughter erupts in the kitchen. It's a weirdly cheery sound.

Amanda's smile is grim as she says, "You already know what I think about coincidences."

# TEN

VINCENT IS in my old room. Or he was supposed to be, anyway. It's weird to go through his things, knowing he never will again. Unlike Jean-Guy, who came with the streamlined luggage of a seasoned traveler, Vincent appears to have arrived under the impression he was moving in. He might have been. Selling hundred-thousand-dollar wine must make good money. He's got two suitcases and a hanging suit bag that appears to be bursting with formalwear. A tuxedo jacket is halfway out of the bag, and as I examine the rest, I find three other jackets and matching pants, along with enough shirts and ties to outfit an entire wedding party.

"Looks like he was planning for quite the event," I say.

"None of this is designer, though," Amanda says, rifling through one of his suitcases.

I snort. "Snob."

"A guy like this has to dress for the job. If he doesn't fit in with his clientele, he'll never sell anything. So it's designer labels, but nothing too flashy. Analogue watch. No jewelry." She holds up a glittering gold link bracelet.

"Like you used to look the part at all those events we used to go to?" I ask, but I check the labels on the jackets, and sure enough, they're all brands I recognize from big box stores and malls.

"Similar. Here he should be dressing to impress but not brag about his money. I was dressing to blend in."

I give her an incredulous glance. Amanda never blended in. She turned heads every time we walked into the room.

"What?" she asks.

"We have very different definitions of blending in. I always felt like a child standing next to you. Like everyone looked at me and assumed you'd bought me a pretty new dress and told me to behave."

Her incredulity melts, but somehow her sympathy is worse. I still feel like a child a lot of the time with her. She might as well pat me on the head and tell me I'm doing a good job pretending to be a detective.

"I was always looking at you," she says.

The compliment makes me flush, and I try to laugh it off. "Yeah, because you were worried I was going to dribble wine on my boobs."

The sympathy turns to heat. Amanda always did have a thing for my tits. No one I've been with since—and it hasn't been many—has given them nearly enough attention.

We both seem to realize now is not the time, though, and glance away. Amanda opens another suitcase. I go to the stack of boxes against the wall. They're all white cartons of the same size, though they're marked with different labels. Macintosh. Mystic Cross. Domaine Meunier Dormant. Wine cases, and inside are a dozen bottles with a variety of labels like the ones in the cellar.

"He said he'd brought some bottles from his private collection," I say as I go through the labels. "They were planning to open some at dinner, and he said some would be included in the sale tomorrow."

"See anything you recognize?"

In the last box, there are eleven bottles, with the twelfth compartment empty.

*Domaine Saint-Arnault. Grand Cru. 1966.*

I must make a noise because Amanda says, "What is it?"

"Here." I hold up the bottle, shining the lantern on it. "It's the same, right?"

She studies it, lower lip between her teeth before she bends and pulls out another one. 1966. In total, there are three from 1966. The rest are from varying years between 1962 and 1971, though there's only one of each of those. The labels on the oldest are yellowed and the topography is less crisp, but it's an entire collection from Domaine Saint-Arnault.

"The answer has to be right here, and I can't see it," I say.

"We have to assume the bottle that was used to hit him came from this case," Amanda says. "Since your dad's collection only had 1965 in it, the broken bottle upstairs must have been the twelfth bottle in this case."

"So whoever killed him came in here, took the wine, then went back out to the dining room and hit him with it?"

"More likely he had it with him when the storm hit, and someone saw the opportunity. If I were going to kill someone, hitting them over the head with a wine bottle isn't the way I'd do it. You'd have to know exactly where to hit and with how much force."

"Yuriy?" I ask. He seems like the kind of dude who would have the skills to murder someone with an improvised weapon.

"The more I think about it, the more I don't think it is him. He wouldn't do it like that. Too visible. Too public."

"But what about them being weird and creepy down on the path to the boathouse? They're up to something."

"They're absolutely here for a reason. But he wouldn't bring his wife here if they'd sent him to kill someone, and he definitely wouldn't have done it as we were about to get hit with a storm. Assassinations, like what you're thinking of, take planning. The timing has to be exact so they can get in and get out without arousing suspicion. If there was any chance of them getting stuck here, they'd have called it off and waited for the next opportunity."

"Unless that's exactly why he did it then," I say, pulse racing as the picture draws itself in my mind. "He wanted to throw off suspicion, so he made it appear like it was an amateur."

She leans in and kisses me. It's so fast I don't even see it coming, and it's over before I realize it happened.

"You're cute when you're excited," she says, and the words are basically a purr.

I pout. "I hate it when people call me cute." I've been called cute my entire life. The joy of being the shortest one in almost any situation.

"Sorry," she murmurs, though she doesn't seem very sorry. "And I get what you're saying about Yuriy, but when in doubt, the simplest explanation is always the most likely. If it looks like Vincent was killed by someone who didn't know what they were doing, and possibly didn't even mean to kill him, that's most likely the truth. The most probable sequence of events is someone saw the chance and hit him."

My head hurts as I struggle to follow what she's saying. How is her version of events simpler than mine? Only one of Sloan's guests is affiliated with organized crime and everyone else is a boring insecure person trying to live their life who may or may not have accidentally killed a wine auctioneer.

"We should get back," she says. "They'll be done eating and getting antsy. We don't want them dispersing."

I yawn so hard my jaw pops. Amanda's lips quirk up in a grin.

"If we let them go to bed, they can't kill each other," I say.

"Unless you want to play hall monitor like we're on a high school field trip, we can't be sure any of them will stay in their assigned rooms."

What a mess.

We go back to the kitchen. Reena and her staff have put together some teeny sandwiches with smoked salmon and dill. A bottle of wine is sitting in the middle of the island, but it's unopened. The label says Ravina, and I can't tell if that's a clue or if I'm seeing conspiracies everywhere now. The others—Sloan and the guests—are all eating and looking sullen.

"Is this the part where you monologue about the sequence of events so far and then randomly accuse one of us of being a murderer, only to have him pull out a gun and say you'll never take him alive?" Chris asks as we walk in.

Amanda gives him a frosty smile. "What do you know about the relationship between Vincent and Jean-Guy?"

The room gets quiet. Yuriy and Lana are like two dark shadows in the corner. They are staring at each other, refusing to acknowledge anyone else. Sloan is still huddled with Bert and Didi. They're all tired. No doubt Didi was here at the crack of dawn helping Sloan arrange flowers or set tables, though all their hard work is crushed under the tree in the dining room. And Chris and Laurel are sitting a less-than-friendly distance apart having a rushed and whispered conversation before Laurel straightens and says, "They hated each other."

"How so?"

"I'm not sure about the details, but Jean-Guy hinted a bit in some of our conversations. About a decade ago, he tried to write a piece alleging that Vincent was hoarding specific wines to drive up their value artificially."

"But that's how all these things work," I say. "Art, diamonds, they're only worth what someone will pay for them, and if they're rare, they're worth more."

She shrugs. "Like I said, I don't know it all. But Jean-Guy was planning something this weekend. I was supposed to get cozy with Vincent and ask him about his personal collection and how he finds so many rare wines. Jean-Guy said once we had proof, I'd be able to write for any publication I wanted."

Chris makes an annoyed sound at the reminder of Laurel's betrayal. Yuriy also huffs out an impatient sound, and Lana has a hand on his arm like she's trying to keep him calm.

"Proof of what?" I ask, but Laurel only shrugs.

"He didn't tell me that. Just something about Vincent's collection."

"So there was bad blood between Vincent and Jean-Guy," Amanda says. "And this was Vincent's auction. So how did Jean-Guy turn up?"

Another silence falls. We all glance around. Finally, Sloan says, "Bert invited him."

I roll my eyes at her childish finger point. Bert's expression widens in surprise, almost like he'd forgotten he was in the room with the rest of us. He stutters for a moment before he says, "I didn't invite him. He reached out to me."

"When was this?" Amanda asks.

"A month ago. He said he was coming to Toronto for an event. He was working on a profile about Vincent and asked if he could come up and speak to some guests." He looks around like he's asking for forgiveness. "I was so flattered when he asked. I've been reading his articles in *Terroir* for years. I didn't think him being here could hurt anyone." A tear slips down his cheek, and he wipes it away. Didi grabs a paper cocktail napkin off the counter and hands it to him to dab at his eyes.

"He didn't mention that he and Vincent had any history?" Amanda asks.

Bert shakes his head and sniffles before he collects himself. "He said he was particularly interested in Vincent's experience with Bordeaux blends. Your father has some nice Bordeaux wines, Gilly. I thought it would be great for everyone."

I ignore his blather. If there was a less-than-friendly history, clearly Jean-Guy was being sneaky for one reason or another. Could he be the one who killed Vincent? Then he jumped off the deck in a moment of remorse? Amanda said to go for the simplest solution, and to me, this would be it. But he went to the trouble of hiding why he was coming and bringing all his research and everything with him, then took the risk of killing Vincent in front of so many potential witnesses; suicide seems unlikely after so much planning.

How do people do this? Solve murders, I mean. I suppose most of the time they have access to resources like phones and the internet so they can do things like question friends and family and get a better idea of who the victims are. They're not groping around in the literal dark looking for clues that could mean anything.

My first plan was a better one. Amanda and I should go back to the boathouse and make out until the sun comes up. If anyone else dies before that, Sloan can deal with it. Three murders in one night would surely mean this place stays in the family for generations, right?

So of course, as I'm about to take Amanda's hand, Yuriy springs to life, snaking an arm out and grabbing hold of one of the kitchen staff. From nowhere, he produces a knife. It's got a long curved blade, like you might use for slicing things very thinly. Things like smoked salmon. But Yuriy's clearly got other ideas as he holds the blade to the terrified cook's throat.

"That's enough bullshit," he snarls. "Get me off this island, or people start dying for real."

# ELEVEN

OH BOY.

"Uhh . . ." I say, which clearly helps the situation.

"Oh my god, don't hurt her!" Sloan says, hands outstretched like that's going to help too.

"My wife and I need to get off this island," Yuriy says. "You have thirty minutes to make it happen, or this woman will pay for your delay."

"My name is Kennedy," the woman against him says. She's got her chin tipped up like she can somehow evade his blade, but she's at least six inches shorter than he is, and his arm across her chest might as well be a tree trunk.

"There's no phone signal," Sloan says. "No boat. Don't you think we all want to get out of here?" Her plea for sympathy is roundly ignored, and I can't really blame Yuriy. The way she phrases it makes it all sound like we're passengers waiting for updates on a delayed flight. Like we're all equally inconvenienced by tonight's events. But the terror in Kennedy's eyes disagrees. We are not all in the same boat.

"What do we do?" I whisper to Amanda.

"Hand-to-hand combat isn't really my specialty."

105

"What about hostage negotiations?"

"That either." But she's tense, like she might leap into action at any second. I want to see her do it. Just because it's not her specialty doesn't mean she can't. How many times has she karate chopped some bad guy in a cloakroom or chased down an assassin in an alley? My imagination is getting away from me again, but there was that one night when we were at yet another fundraising dinner where she disappeared for about half an hour after the first course. When she came back, she said she'd had to take an urgent work call, but knowing what I know now, it wasn't some C-suite executive with a crisis.

Movement comes out of the corner of my eye. It's Chris, launching himself into the air and letting out a barbarian scream. It might be terrifying in a loincloth, but in his khakis and collared shirt, it's out of place, and it doesn't go the way he'd hoped. Instead of taking Yuriy by surprise and tackling him, he gets knocked aside like an annoying bug. Laurel cries out as Chris hits the kitchen island. When he staggers upright, his sleeve has a slice in it, and red seeps out along the material.

"You stabbed me," he says, sounding shocked, like he'd never considered this possibility. He puts his fingers on the wound and stares at the glistening blood on them. "You fucking stabbed me."

"You deserved it for being so foolish," Yuriy says, but Chris must not hear him before taking one stumbling step backward as he continues to gape at his stained fingers and then collapses on the floor.

"Chris!" Laurel is at his side in a second. He's more or less fainted, which seems about right. She cradles his head in her lap, and one of the non-hostage kitchen staff hands her a tea towel to press against his arm, which wakes him up again in a hurry as he cries out.

"Those are linen!" Sloan says, staring at the towel.

"Oh, for god's sake. You're really worried about laundry right now?" I ask.

"Enough!" Yuriy's still got Kennedy, and he tightens his hold on her, making her grab at his arm like she's having a hard time breathing. "You have twenty-eight minutes. A boat, or I kill the woman."

"We don't have a boat," Sloan says. "I sold it."

"We do," Bert says.

"You don't," I say. "The lines snapped in the storm, remember?"

"We have another one. The tinny. Back at the house. I can go get it."

"How?" I ask.

He fumbles for words, but finally, he says, "I can swim across."

"That's ridiculous," I say. "It's too dark." Even in daylight, I don't think he could do it. Bert's older than my dad, and he has enjoyed his retired life of luxury for decades. He loves good food and wine, and he is not an athlete unless you count the way he screams at the TV while watching Wimbledon. The swim to Channel Island is two or three hundred meters.

"I'll go," Didi says.

"No, pumpkin, I can't ask you to do that," Bert says.

"Pssh, don't be silly. I swam twice that far for the osteoporosis charity relay last month." She pats his cheek. Didi's always participating in those kinds of events. The walk to end childhood poverty. The big swim for heart disease. The bigger swim to save all our asses.

"It's risky," Amanda says.

"Twenty-seven minutes," Yuriy says.

"Why do you suddenly need off this island so badly?" I ask. "You've been here for hours, and suddenly you're all 'Do as I say if you want to live'?" For the last part, I try to mimic his Eastern

European accent, but it comes out so muddled that I probably sound Jamaican or something. Yuriy scowls like a thundercloud. Amanda puts a warning hand on my arm.

"I can do it," Didi says, sounding confident, even though the task sounds impossible. She may be fit, but she's over seventy, and in her cottage chic wardrobe, I can't see how this is our best option.

"How do we know you'll even come back?" Laurel asks from the floor where she's still holding Chris. His eyes are closed, but I'd put money on the fact he's not unconscious, only faking it until the immediate threat has passed.

"I will accompany her," Lana says, making all our heads turn. "I will swim with her and bring the boat back for Yuriy."

"I'll go too," I say, before I can give it a second thought. Yuriy is strong and intimidating, but Lana's gaze on the room is like ice, and with everything that has happened tonight, I wouldn't put it past her to go with Didi, find the boat, then kill her. She needs backup, and it's not like we can send Sloan.

"Gil, that's not a good idea," Amanda says.

"It's fine. I can get the tinny started. Didi will need help if there's debris on the island."

"Then I'll go with you."

"No." Yuriy's voice booms through the kitchen, making us jump. "You stay here. If you go, you will find a way to alert the authorities."

"Don't you think she'd have done that already if she could?" I ask. Amanda's hand on my arm is so tight now my fingers tingle as she cuts off the circulation. I shrug her off. "Didi and I will go. Lana will come if you think that's necessary. We'll be back as soon as we can." Twentyish minutes will be very tight, and we really have to pray the tin fishing boat Bert's talking about isn't stuck under a fallen tree.

There's a moment where we're all engaged in a stare-off like we've left Muskoka and gone straight to the OK Corral. Lana mutters something low to Yuriy. Laurel is dabbing Chris's brow with a clean corner of the ruined tea towel. Didi gives Bert's arm a reassuring pat. Finally, Yuriy says, "Yes. Get the boat."

As plans go, this is a terrible one, but we gotta do what we can. I get life jackets for everyone from the little shed. When I slide mine on, there's a sensation like water running the wrong way, going up my spine instead of down. It's undoubtedly a spider trying to make an escape from his polystyrene home. I shudder, even if I can't see it.

"Are you sure you can do this?" Amanda asks. We're in the middle of a weird procession down to the waterline. Yuriy still has a hold on Kennedy's arm while he grasps the knife in his other hand. The others are ahead and behind us. Even Chris has roused himself for the upcoming spectacle, though he leans heavily on Laurel the whole way down. I suppose it's better than the alternative Yuriy proposed, which was to lock everyone in the wine cellar. The very idea was too claustrophobic to bear. So we go down to the lake like a line of obedient ducklings. Yuriy and Lana have another conversation. Bert and Didi say their goodbyes in hushed, hurried words. The click of the buckles as I do up my life jacket seems very loud. We're all still in our clothes, so we can't inspire much confidence for the people we're leaving behind, but we're what it's come to.

At the last second, before I step to the top of the ladder, Amanda grabs my wrist and pulls me so hard I nearly fall off the dock onto the sandy beach below.

"What are you doing?"

She knows exactly what she's doing. Her lips on mine are a question and a promise at the same time. I answer her with the same.

"Be careful," she says. The lantern is on the dock, and a few people have their phone lights on, though batteries have started to die. But down here, Amanda and I are mostly in shadow.

"I will," I say.

"If you can find a way to get word to the police or anyone else on shore, that would be best."

"I can't risk Didi," I say.

"I understand." She kisses me again. "But come back, okay? There are things we need to talk about."

My heart swells. Things to talk about. Things we should have talked about six years ago. Things I've missed every day since.

"I have to tell you," I say, "this spy life might be a little too much for me."

"This is nothing like my spy life," she says. "I told you that's mostly meetings and emails to other spies who spend their days in meetings too."

"Relaxing." I take her hand in mine. "You'll have to show me sometime."

"Gilly?" Didi calls. She's already in the water. "Are you coming? It's okay if you changed your mind. I'll be all right."

Just Didi and the murder ballerina swimming off into the darkness. I can't let that happen.

"I'm coming!" I say, with a final squeeze of Amanda's hand. "I'll be right back. Promise."

She kisses me one more time, but finally, I have to pull myself away. I gasp as the water closes over my ankles. The fabric of my pants clings to me as it soaks through. I hiss when gentle waves splash over my thighs and up my crotch. When we were in our late teens or early twenties, Sloan and I used to call this the labia line and squealed every time we tried to go for a swim. I miss that version of my sister.

The clouds have cleared enough that a sliver of moonlight shines down on the water. I can see Didi's bright white hair and swim toward her, nearly colliding with the darker shape of Lana as I approach.

"You okay, Gilly?" Didi asks.

It's such a simple question. Motherly, almost. And there's no way to answer it in the time we have, so all I say is, "Yup. Let's go."

We start to swim.

# TWELVE

THE GOOD NEWS IS, the water isn't as cold as it could be—by Canadian standards, anyway. In late summer, it's had lots of time to heat up under the sun.

The dark is completely disorienting, though. We can't be more than a few feet away from the dock before the cell phone lights dwindle to pinpoints like stars. The lantern glows, but someone picks it up, and the sight of it bobbing free in the air makes the whole world seem like it's about to tilt sideways and I have to close my eyes.

Something brushes against me, and I shriek involuntarily.

"Shh, Gilly." It's Didi.

"I can't see anything." Panic rises in my throat. I didn't realize how much I'm used to small lights, even at night, out here. An exterior light on someone's deck. The glow of a fire in a pit by the beach. The motion sensor light at the end of a dock that comes on whenever a branch waves in front of it. Tonight, there's none of that.

"It's okay." She takes my hand. "Stick with me."

"Is everyone okay?" Amanda calls from shore, and every instinct tells me to swim toward her.

"We can do this," Didi says. "They need us to help them."

They do. And Didi needs me.

"I'm fine!" I call out.

Ahead, someone is splashing in the water. Lana. I have a brief mental flash of swimming up behind her and trying to pull her under. Out here in the dark, no one would be able to help her. But I don't have it in me, no matter what the danger is. I can't kill someone. And even if I could, Lana would fight back. I'd likely wind up being the one drowned instead of her.

Suddenly, the sky glows red above us. It's sudden enough to set off a new wave of panic in my chest, and my limbs go wobbly as I try to keep going.

"Good man," Didi says.

It's a flare, the kind used to signal from a boat in distress. Bert must have found them in the boathouse. The light lasts a few seconds, but it's enough to orient us. Lana's twenty feet in front, her pale dress streaming behind her like a mermaid's tail. Bert and Didi's dock is farther to the right than I thought. I kick, trying to get myself headed in the right direction as the light fades. When the dark returns, it's not as bad as before. The space in front of me is inky, but there are little details now. A flash of white over rippling water. Little wobbling specks of light that might be fireflies close to shore. I want the flare to come again, but there can't be many of them. We'll need one to find our way back, and hopefully, Bert knows that.

My muscles ache. I focus on the sound of Didi and Lana ahead of me. If I get in trouble, they won't be able to find me to help. My clothes aren't heavy, but soaked through with water, every kick takes so much more work than I can give.

Another flare glows overhead, just in time for me to see I'm about to swim directly into a tree that floats silently through the lake. I splash as I try to kick away from it without losing my sense of direction. The dock is so much closer than I thought. Lana's already climbing the swim ladder.

Didi is nowhere in sight.

How many seconds of light left?

I push at the water, trying to turn. Did she fall behind me? I'd have heard her go by, right?

At the last moment, I see her white head pop up from the water. She's front crawling her way parallel to the shore, away from the dock.

"Didi!" I call. There's a fraction of a second before the world goes dark again. I tread water for what seems like an age, gasping as I strain to listen for more of her rhythmic stroke as she gets further away from us.

But her voice comes over the water. "I got it."

The ladder rattles against the dock. I follow the sound, groping for the cold metal. As I climb, I can almost make out the shapes of Didi and Lana on the dock.

"You okay?" Didi asks.

"Yeah." I'm out of breath, and there's a raw spot under my arm where the life jacket rubbed while I dog paddled, but I'm here and that's what matters. "I wish there was a way to tell them we made it."

A sharp whistle pierces the dark. It's so loud, I drop to the boards. A splinter lodges itself in my palm.

Didi chuckles. "That was very impressive."

"Thank you," Lana says in that same soft voice that's always a surprise.

"My daughter can whistle like that."

An echoing whistle comes from the direction we've come.

Lana says, "Yuriy taught me," and she and Didi both laugh. Their footsteps thud softly as they talk. They sound like old friends catching up on stories. I do my best to hurry after them, trying to remember if the dock curves to the left or right before it gets to the shore. When my feet hit solid ground, I stumble again.

"Gilly, are you coming?" Didi asks.

"Trying to," I say.

"Come on, there's a flashlight in the boathouse. That way we'll be able to see what we're doing."

Of course, like everywhere else tonight, getting into the boathouse is no joke. It was damaged in the storm, and the door is jammed. In the end, I have to get back in the water, swim around the outside, and scramble up the framing inside the slip where Bert and Didi's lost sailboat should go. I acquaint myself with what is no doubt several nests of spiders in the process, and I've never considered myself to have phobias per se, but that might be changing very soon. Once I'm up, I throw my shoulder against the door while Didi and Lana pull from the outside. Finally, we get it open. Didi moves about confidently, even in the dark, and shortly after, I'm wincing as she shines a boxy yellow plastic flashlight directly into my eyes.

"There you are," she says with a pleased smile as she undoes her life jacket. She's soaked. The bow at her neck is drooping, and a dark-coloured bra shows through the wet material of her white blouse. "Come on, let's put on something dry before we head back."

"We're running out of time," I say. "Kennedy. She needs—" I struggle with how to phrase it in a way that doesn't make me jittery. I'm beyond exhausted. My brain is running a hundred percent on instinct and adrenaline.

Lana makes an amused sound. "Yuriy won't hurt anyone."

I round on her. "What do you mean?"

"I'm sorry," Didi says. "When we invited you, we didn't think there would be so much trouble."

"Trouble?"

Lana shrugs. "It was a risk, but Yuriy loves the Famille Bonnehumeur Cote du Rhone, and it is very hard to find."

"The famille who?"

"You should have let Bert buy it for you like we offered." Didi gives Lana's shoulder a friendly bump, and my head spins.

What the motherfucking hell is going on?

They both swing their attention toward me.

"Gilly," Didi gasps. "That's no way to speak in front of a guest."

Did I say that out loud?

I scrub at my eyes. "I'm really sorry. It's probably all the murder and sleeplessness, but I don't understand what's going on right now at all."

They give each other knowing smiles that make me want to fling the flashlight into the lake so I don't have to see them anymore.

"I invited Yuriy and Lana to come for the auction," Didi says, like it's the most obvious answer in the world.

"And here I thought they came for the horse show," I say.

"Don't be silly, Gilly. There are no horses."

They both turn to squeeze through the crooked door.

"Wait," I say, trailing after them. "What do you mean you invited them? You know people like . . ." I almost say people like *them* in a way that makes it clear exactly what I think of Yuriy and Lana. And let's be fair, the opinion is deserved, what with the lurking in the trees and threatening the staff. But the way Didi keeps throwing friendly smiles suggests she may not share my opinion.

"Lana and I met at a fundraiser in Paris last summer," Didi says, clearly oblivious to the tension between me and Lana. "She had choreographed a performance with Olivier Fernando. You know him."

I scoff. "Who doesn't?" No idea who Olivier Fernando is,

but unless he killed someone in Muskoka tonight, it's beside the point.

"Of course you do," Didi says approvingly. "Lana, Olivier, and I got to talking, and I mentioned that Bert had gone to a tasting at Chez les Dauphins instead of coming to the gala, and Lana said that Yuriy was also a wine collector. One thing led to another, and here we are."

*Here we are.* The ground might as well drop out from under me and send me plummeting into the void. Didi and the murder ballerina are friends? Does that mean she's not a murder ballerina? Or did Didi get mixed up in some kind of scam? What if all her charitable endeavors are more money laundering?

"But what's with all the 'Get me a boat or the girl gets it'?" I ask. At least my Russian accent is better this time. "If you're only here for wine, and you didn't kill anyone—"

Didi laughs like it's the most hysterical thing she's heard all night. "Of course they didn't kill anyone. Chris killed Vincent and Jean-Guy. Who else could it be? No one else knew both of them or had a reason to hurt anyone."

Please excuse me while I go drown myself in the lake. I can't even begin to think critically about what's happening here. There's a wooden Muskoka chair by the door, and I slump into it, my knees basically giving out. I need Amanda. Amanda would understand what's happening. Or would at least have the wherewithal to get answers faster than I can, apparently.

"We have to get them away before anyone comes in the morning. They were only supposed to be here for the evening," Didi says. She doesn't seem to notice my distress at all as she fumbles in the rock garden at the corner of the house. "They were going to offer Vincent twice the price for the Famille Bonnehumeur, and then Bert would sail them back to the marina once you'd all gone to bed. They have to keep a low profile. Because of what Yuriy does. Now where is that spare key?" She waves the flashlight around.

"What does Yuriy do?" I ask.

"Oh, here it is." Didi holds up a shiny silver key on a pink fob. She glances at Lana. "Can we tell her? Gilly can keep a secret. She never told Bert about that time she saw me kissing Magnus Robbie after the yacht club potluck in 2012. Did you, Gilly? Too many rum and cokes." She gives me a wink. Honestly, I'd forgotten about her and Magnus. I'd found them more than kissing. More like he'd had his hand up her skirt in the cabin of Bert's power cruiser. She'd found me later and told me it was "just between us girls." It had been years before I'd been able to look Bert in the eye again, but either he'd never found out or he had and didn't care. Pretty sure Magnus had retired to Norway not long after, anyway.

Lana sighs. "If you think it's necessary."

Didi does, clearly deciding it is. "Yuriy's a spy. He's a double agent for the Americans in Belarus."

I laugh. It's a high, giddy sound. "A spy. Of course he is. Everyone is tonight."

Didi pats my shoulder. "Yes. That's pretty shocking about Amanda. You never had any idea while you were together? It must have been so exciting."

She doesn't wait for a reply. Instead, she unlocks the front door and disappears inside with Lana right behind her. For a minute, I think about staying where I am. I don't need dry clothes. I need a tranquillizer. Honestly, a wine bottle to the head would be fine right now. A few hours of sleep away from all these revelations is the only thing that will bring me back to reality.

So of course, a scream echoes inside. Didi. I shouldn't have left her alone.

I spring to my feet and rush inside, ready to do battle with whatever waits.

# THIRTEEN



"DIDI? DIDI?"

Almost immediately I stub my toe on something. Table. Shelf. Who the hell knows? I curse and call out again.

"I'm okay," Didi says. The glow of the flashlight bobs back into view, around a corner in the hall. "Just knocked over some of Bert's collection. That's a shame. The '63 was going to pay for our trip to Dubai this winter. But he should have put it back in the cellar instead of leaving it here on the table."

I dodge the sofa and find Lana and Didi looking down at a shattered bottle of wine.

"Domaine Saint-Arnault?" I say, examining the label.

Didi nods eagerly. "It's Bert's favourite. He's bought so much from Vincent. We call it our retirement fund, even though we're already retired. '64, '65, and '67 are the best years."

"Not '66?" I dodge around the puddle and broken glass as they walk up the hall.

"There is no '66," she says. "There was an infection. Mould. They lost the whole crop that year. That's why the '67 is so valuable. It's nearly impossible to find, but Bert has bought three of them from Vincent's auctions. He's very proud of himself.

Don't get him started when we get back to the house, or he'll talk your ear off all night. He planned to buy the ones from your dad, though I guess we'll have to figure out something new since Vincent is dead." She says it like Vincent's let them down personally. There's something there in what she just said. My tired mind struggles to piece it together. No '66. But there is. It's at the house. Amanda and I saw it. The bloody one by Vincent's body, and more like it in his room. He'd said he had a big surprise. Was that it? Bottles of a wine that's not supposed to exist?

Didi leads us to her bedroom, and we change into dry clothes. We're like the aftermath of a British bedroom comedy. Lana is significantly taller than Didi, so the linen pants she's given barely reach past her calves. By comparison, Didi hands me a pair of Bermuda shorts that also reach my calves.

Back near the water, the tinny is half full of rainwater that needs to be bailed out before we can push it down the rocky beach. Lana lets out another one of her screaming whistles, and an echoing response comes as we get the little outboard motor going. With a growling whine, it propels us across the lake, and we're more than halfway there when a fresh flare shoots into the sky, lighting our way. They're all still there. Bert, Sloan, Yuriy. Amanda. My heart beats too quickly in my chest as we come alongside the dock. We're going faster than ideal, but with only the yellow flashlight and the lantern on the dock to orient us, it's a forgivable offence.

"Oops," Didi says with a careless grin.

It's everything I can do not to throw myself into Amanda's arms as we step off the tinny and onto the dock. She must see it in my face, though, because she puts an arm around my shoulders, holding me close.

"Everything okay?" she asks.

I blink back tears I wasn't expecting to cry. "I'll tell you later."

Yuriy joins Lana in the tinny. Didi gives them the flashlight, which is hardly going to help them at all. The channels between some of the islands are narrow and no doubt clogged with fallen branches and debris from the storm. If they somehow make it back to town without crashing, it will be a miracle.

Also, though, not my problem. Either they killed Vincent and Jean-Guy and are making their escape, in which case we're all safe and have nothing more pressing to do but sleep or drink until the sun comes up. Or else they didn't, the killer is still here, and the list of suspects just got significantly smaller.

I don't like being a spy. Give me my desk job back.

The whine of the outboard disappears into the dark. One by one, everyone returns to the house. Soon, it's only me and Amanda on the dock. The world is so quiet we could be the only two people in it.

She slides her hand into mine. "What happened?"

"They didn't kill them," I say, before realizing that sentence is unhelpfully vague. "Yuriy and Lana. They didn't kill anyone. At least not here. He works for the Americans."

Amanda makes an intrigued noise but doesn't comment on the last part. Probably she'll report it back to her handler or her superior or whoever she has when she goes back to her spy place.

"I didn't think they did," she says simply, giving me a squeeze. "Like I told you. It wouldn't make sense—"

"It's not fair." I wheel on her before she can spout more nonsense about how wise she is when it comes to things like criminals and motives and opportunities.

Her hand squeezes tighter around mine. "What isn't?"

"You. You're not being fair. You waltz in here all beautiful and perfect and all 'Oh, by the way, I have this sexy spy job I wasn't allowed to tell you about,' and you act like everything's okay. Like we never broke up and that you get to touch me and tell me things now, when that's all I ever wanted." My voice is rising. They can probably hear me at the house. Let them. "But it's too late, Amanda. You left and I was alone. I got fired. Did you know that? After we broke up, I was a mess for six months. They finally told me not to come back to work, so I didn't. I lay in bed for another month before Sloan pitched a fit that I was worrying Dad and she couldn't handle that. Because she has to be the centre of attention. It can't be me. I can't be the one people worry about. It has to be her, like it's her who decides when we sell this place and sell off Dad's things and . . ." The words run out in a strangled sob, and she pulls me to her, wrapping me up in a hug while I cry into her chest. It's exactly the thing I just told her I don't want, but that's a lie and we both know it. She's all I've ever wanted. I didn't want the secrets. The lies. The half-truths and the long silences where I was left to fill in the blanks.

She's running her hands down my back and muttering, "I'm sorry. I'm sorry," in my hair. I can't stop the tears that soak through her shirt. And I can't stop when I reach up and pull her face down to mine. Her kiss is tentative, but she won't refuse me.

"Gil," she says softly.

"Please," I say. "Just tonight. It's not too late. Please."

I wish we could stumble up the dock, tangling fingers and mouths and everything else like we used to. But it's fucking dark out, and I've already been in the lake once. So we do that awkward thing lovers do when they're about to have sex but have to be all businesslike for a few more moments. We walk silently to the boathouse. Amanda carries the lantern, and I fiddle with the hem of my borrowed shirt. I'm sweating.

Nervous. So fucking turned on, and we've hardly done anything yet.

But I must not be the only one who is a mess of feelings and hormones, because the second we're in the loft, she's on me. Pushing me down to the bed, with one knee planted between my thighs. This time there's no hesitation in my kiss. It's exactly like I want. Like I remembered. I push her off long enough to peel out of Didi's shirt and shorts. They're not mine, and I don't want anyone or anything else between us. She follows in quick fashion, stripping down to the lacy bra and panty set I knew she'd be wearing underneath. I always gave her a hard time for those. Told her they were silly. That she was giving in to the patriarchy or something like that. She'd laugh and tell me they were pretty. And they are. Even in the dim propane-fueled light around us, she's beautiful, raised up on her knees so I can see every inch of her.

"Is that a tattoo?" My eyes widen as I stroke the dark blue ink that peeks out over the silky band of her underwear.

She bites her lip and pulls it down far enough to show the whole thing. It's a single feather, curved and at an angle like it's drifting on an invisible current of air.

"When did you get this?" I ask, running a thumb over it gently. I'm afraid to touch it, like I might break up the downy softness so the little threads, or whatever they're called, never lie together the same way again. Like us. It'll never be the same, but that doesn't mean it's a bad idea. Not tonight, anyway.

Since she's so obligingly started the process, I pull her underwear down the rest of the way. The material is so soft and cool between my fingers, but her skin beneath is blazing hot. I slide a finger between the folds of her labia, and she's already wet.

"Gilly," she says. Her eyes are closed and her hips shift restlessly even though I'm barely touching her. It was always like this. Maybe this is all it was. Great sex and comfort. But there are worse things to build a relationship on, right?

Nope. That's the wrong train of thought. I told her that it wasn't too late. That there was time. What I meant was that we still had time before sunrise. Not that there was time for us. A future. All we have is tonight. I hope she knows that. She must, right?

But while I'm musing pointless questions about the relationship we left behind years ago, Amanda has taken control and is riding my hand. She's taken hold of my wrist and is rocking against my fingers. Her lower lip is between her teeth, and she is beautiful. Purposeful. She always knew what she wanted and took it. But I should help. It's the considerate thing to do, regardless of who we'll be—or won't be—to each other in the morning. With my thumb, I find the nub of her clit, flicking at it before turning it in small circles. She moans, and my fingers get slicker. She wants this. Wants me. That's all that matters in this moment.

"Come here," I say, pulling her down to kiss her. She follows my lead willingly, rolling as I turn us so I'm on top and can wriggle out of my undergarments. She cups my breasts, squeezing and kneading them before she pinches one of the nipples, then rises up to kiss away the sting. I wrap my legs around her, tangling my fingers in her hair. This, with me up on my knees and her leaning back against the wall, is the only way I can be taller than her. We learned all the tricks back then to make us fit together. But the real answer might be that we never fit at all.

Still, for tonight we can pretend.

"This would work better with a headboard," she says, kissing farther down my body. She roams over my stomach while sliding her hands to my hips, pulling me forward and showing me where to settle, even though I need no instruction at all.

Her tongue on my clit has my whole body igniting like a flame to a wick. The sound that comes out of my throat is half-familiar and half-forgotten. It's been such a long time since anyone knew exactly how and where to touch me to turn me on like this.

As she said, there's no headboard, but I plant my palms against the rough wood of the wall. Her grip is strong anyway, so there's no chance of me falling as she licks and sucks. If I had something to hold on to, she might add a finger or two, sliding farther inside of me than her tongue can reach, but it doesn't matter. No one has ever been as good at this as Amanda is, and she moans as I grind against her mouth, spreading my knees a little wider to give her more room to explore.

When I come, my whole body arches back. Just like they could hear me yelling from the dock before, anyone who happens to be still awake can probably hear me now, but I don't care. Amanda holds on, sucking my clit and pulling every last spasm and shudder from my body until I go limp and only her arms around me keep me from crashing on top of her.

She lays me down alongside her. I twitch as the heat of orgasm fades away. She's kissing me. Telling me she's sorry and that I'm beautiful and all the things I want to hear and don't at the same time. So instead, I slide closer so we're face-to-face, then slide my hand between her thighs, touching her like I did before. She's even wetter now, and her breath comes out in a hiss as I stroke.

"Gil," she says, her voice hoarse.

"Wait," I say. "Let me do this."

But she puts her hand over mine, forcing me to still.

"No," she says, kissing me one more time. "Let me. Watch."

So I do. Amanda was never one for putting on a show. It was

part of the excitement. Because sometimes the need was too much to wait until we got home, so we had to be satisfied with whatever we could have in a hall or a back room. Now, though, she takes her time, teasing herself while her gaze is locked on mine. She's so beautiful. So everything.

"I missed you," she says. "Missed the taste of you."

"I know." I can't help myself. I reach for her, covering her hand with mine. The curly hairs between her thighs tickle my fingers.

"I'm sorry," she says. She's breathing harder. If we had more light, I'd be able to see the way the flush is creeping from her chest, up her long throat and to her cheeks. It always does when she gets close.

I kiss her, running my tongue over her bottom lip before nipping at it. She whimpers. I bite again, a little harder. She trades places with me, wrapping her hand over mine, letting me touch and bring her to the edge.

"Good," I say, because she always liked the praise. "You're doing so good."

She shakes her head, fighting it, knowing we're nearly through.

"Gillian."

"Good girl. You're so close, aren't you? You missed me. No one else knows this. How you like it."

In fact, in the end, she's doing it all herself. She rocks her hips against me, finding everything she needs and taking it for herself. I kiss her one last time, holding her head against mine so the only way she can breathe is in great gasps from her nose. I growl once, low, and she goes tight, pushing herself as close as she can. Amanda makes a high squeaking sound against my lips, almost like she's holding back a sob of her own. Then she's shaking and tears her mouth away from me long enough to cry out. She pulls me on top of her, then the blanket over top both of us, and wraps her arms around me.

"I missed you so much," she says, her voice heavy with bliss.

"Yeah," I say, swirling trails only I can see on her skin. "I missed you too."

I'll miss her more when the sun is up and we're off this island because out there is the real world, the one where she can't tell me the truth. And I don't want to live with secrets.

I'll miss this hidden place where we're together more than I can say.

# FOURTEEN

WE MIGHT SLEEP. Who knows how long when it's dark all the time? The battery on my phone is dead, and Amanda's is somewhere in the pockets of the clothes she cast aside.

"So they knew each other all along?" she says. I've been catching her up on the things I learned with Didi and Lana.

"Seems like it," I say.

She's got an arm around my shoulder, and I've got my cheek pressed to her chest. It's comfortable. If we were in a hotel room, this would be luxurious. Here, with the dim camping lantern and the spiders, it's rustic at best.

"There was another thing," I say. "Bert has a bunch of the same wine. Domaine Saint-Arnault. But there was none from 1966. Didi said that wine doesn't exist."

Amanda laughs. It's a heavy, sleepy sound. "They're in for a surprise when they check Vincent's room."

My eyelids droop. Vincent's room. No doubt when this is all over, there will be all kinds of tributes to him and discussion about what the wine community has lost. The magic touch. Finding the unfindable.

"It would have been quite the event tomorrow." I yawn.

Who cares about dead bodies and murderers? We're safe. Let the police handle it in the morning. "Dad's collection is impressive, by the sounds of it. Add in a crown jewel like a wine that isn't supposed to exist. It would have been a lot of money. I can't believe people spend so much on something they can't even drink."

The room falls into silence except for the soft lapping of water in the boat slip below. This is nice. Even if it's not forever, it can be for tonight. That's enough for me.

Amanda sits up suddenly, making me tumble to the thin mattress. I groan my protest.

"Say it again," she says.

"What?" I'm not saying anything. Now is for sleep. Instead, I pull the pillow over my head, but Amanda snatches it away again.

"The wine that doesn't exist. The '66. Tell me again."

I do. There's not much to say. A winery. A fungus. A missing year. It all sounds very tedious.

But the more I talk, the faster Amanda moves. She scrambles out of bed, groping for clothes and struggling into them.

"What are you doing?" I ask.

"There was something in Jean-Guy's notes." She slides her pants over her hips, taking away the view of her silky ass, and I'm so annoyed I said anything at all.

"Where are you going?" I ask. Despite myself, I'm already looking for clothes too. Obviously, Amanda is going to the house. The one with two dead bodies and a murderer, though I agree with Didi that it's most likely Chris, and he doesn't seem to have the guts to actually attack someone outright. He's the kind to clobber you over the head with a priceless bottle of wine or push you off an already shaky balcony. Asshole. I hope Laurel dumps him the second they get home.

"Do you remember? Something about case counts?"

"Cases of what?" I stumble around. "Where the hell is my other shoe?"

"Wine, Gilly," she laughs, then throws the very same shoe in my direction. I fumble and drop down to the bed to catch it. "Cases of wine. Wine that doesn't exist."

"But it does exist," I say. "It literally killed him."

She laughs again. It's a high, excited sound. "That's not the half of it. Come on." She grabs the lantern, and her eyes glisten with excitement. My breath catches. This. I want her to always look at me like this. Uncovered. Unfiltered. There was always something so smooth and polished about her. Flawless, even. The reasons are obvious now. If we were to see each other again, this is the version of Amanda I would want to be with. And she can't give me that.

I follow her up the path to the house. She moves quickly on the uneven ground, and I have to focus what little tired brain-power I have left on keeping up. At the top of the stairs, the house is dark. Everyone else must have had the same idea I did. Okay . . . not the sexy bits. But hopefully, everyone decided to cut their losses and call it a night.

We creep through the empty kitchen and down the hall to the bedrooms. The doors to most are closed, but Jean-Guy's is open, and we slip inside. Amanda closes the door quietly behind us, then goes for the leather-bound notebook I had earlier. She flips through the pages.

"Here," she says, pointing at a page. "Look at this."

"What am I looking at? My French hasn't improved since before."

"This. These columns. On the left is how much wine Domaine Saint-Arnault made each year. And the right is the number of cases Vincent has sold."

I follow the numbers as she indicates them. The number on the left is clearly marked for each. The column on the right is messier. Numbers penciled in and crossed out. Question marks and scribbles.

"I don't see it," I say. "Why is this important?"

She traces the line, starting in the midfifties and working forward. In 1966, the left column has a zero. The right only has a question mark. But before I can say anything, Amanda's tracing back up to the fifties. "Here, he's sold a few of the oldest bottles. But the newer ones, he's sold a bigger and bigger percentage of the total amount that was ever made."

"So? Wouldn't the older ones be harder to find? And the ones from the sixties are worth more, right? So he'd be more interested in selling those."

"But the people who have them would be less likely to want to sell them. Wine that valuable you sell one or two at a time. He's sold *cases*. Dozens. That's potentially millions of dollars."

I nod. "That is how math works, yeah, I get it. He's got the magic touch. He finds the unfindable. That's what Bert said. It's the whole reason he's here."

She shakes her head. "But what if they're not real? None of them. What if the '66 isn't the only wine he's found that doesn't really exist?"

I slump on the bed, head between my hands. It's way too late for riddles.

"Explain it to me like I'm five," I say. "That's all I can handle right now."

She's still scanning the book like it might reveal more secrets. If she keeps this up much longer, I'm going to tell her to wake me up when she's solved the crime. But she suddenly slams the notebook shut with such a resounding snap that I jump. The adrenaline wakes me up again, if only for a little bit. I rub at my eyes.

"Go to the cellar," she says.

"What about you?"

"I'll meet you there."

She presses the notebook to my chest. "Take this and go. Be quiet. Don't wake anyone up. I'll be right there."

I don't like splitting up. Even with Yuriy and Lana gone, there's still a fear like a knife-wielding fiend could leap out from behind a corner at any moment. But she hands me the lantern and disappears soundlessly up the hall, toward the other rooms, and after another moment, I turn and head the other way. I wince at every creak and groan of the floorboards, but the house remains silent otherwise.

In the cellar, I set the lantern on the shelf next to the bottles we pulled out before. Each one is identical except for the year on the label. I go back through Jean-Guy's notebook, cross-referencing the bottles here and the numbers Amanda found before. It's a tidy little sum. Enough that Sloan would have been satisfied and wouldn't have insisted on selling this place.

The clink of glass has me turning. Amanda is a looming shape in the doorway, blocked by the light with my shadow. When I step aside, she's carrying one of the boxes from Vincent's room.

"Great," she says as she sets it down at my feet. "Help me with these."

We pull the bottles from the case. Amanda lines them up in order of date. Dad's all have the paper tags around the neck with careful notes in his handwriting. Otherwise, the bottles are all identical, and the years match up exactly. Except for the 1966 bottles. Amanda has them set in a line a little separate from the others. We're back to staring at inanimate wine bottles like they're about to confess to everything.

She shakes her head. "Impossible."

"What is?"

"They're the same."

"And?"

Amanda grimaces, cocking her head like she's studying a piece of art.

"*Are* they the same?" she asks.

I sigh. She's not going to let this go. I step forward, bringing the lantern with me. I line up the matching bottles side by side and study them carefully. Depending on which way I hold the lantern, Dad's note tags cast a shadow, so I pull each one off and stuff them in my pocket, then check again.

Identical. I'm not even sure what I'm looking for, but if I saw these on the shelf at the store, I wouldn't give them a second glance. Everything from the faded yellow of the label to the lettering on the name is exactly the same. The trees bow toward the big stone home on a hill. Side by side. The same.

At least, that much is true for the first few. The ones bottled in the fifties.

"Here." I tap my finger against the bottle from 1961.

"What?" Amanda is by my side in an instant.

"The ink is smudged."

It's subtle. Hardly worth even noticing, but I've proofed enough designs from the printer to know. If you really squint, the last two letters of *Arnault* on the bottle from Vincent's collection are slightly faded, the delineation between the edges of the scrolling *L* and *T* not quite as crisp as on Dad's bottle.

"A misprint? A bad roll of labels?" Amanda says, but she leans in closer.

"It's the same here," I say, looking at 1962, then '63. "And here."

My pulse thumps in my throat. This is important. Critical, in fact. This little defect in the label is about to tell us everything we've been trying to figure out.

"What are the odds they bought labels from someone who had the same mistake in their printer three years in a row? And that only Vincent bought those same bottles, while your dad's are all fine?" Amanda says. She's placed one hand in the middle of my back, and her fingers drum an agitated rhythm against my spine.

"Four years," I say, moving farther up the row.

"Gilly." She hisses air through her teeth.

1965 is the same. So is 1967. That one imperfection the only trace that all might not be as it seems. Each of the labels on Dad's bottles remains clear and perfect, even with the passage of time. Each of Vincent's is not.

We come to the bottles from 1966. Amanda spaces them out so we can examine each carefully. I can hardly make out the details anymore. Like reading the same word over and over until it's lost all meaning. But Amanda brings over the first of Dad's bottles from 1951, and the difference is immediately clear once you know what to look for.

"What does it mean?" I ask.

"What if . . ." she says slowly, tapping on her bottom lip now, "you were in the business of selling very expensive wine. But you also had a very expensive wine collection of your own. How would you fund it?"

"I'd sell more wine than I buy," I say, but already I can see the flaw in that.

"But what if there's a limited supply of wine to sell?" Amanda says. She's shaking. Vibrating. The bracelets at her wrist jingle as her tapping fingers pick up speed. "You can only ever make so much money because most of the wine is already in private collections where it's going to disappear into cellars for decades. The only way to make more money is to find new wine. To find—"

"The unfindable wines." I take hold of one of the '66s, staring down at the nearly perfect label.

"Or make them yourself." She takes the bottle from me, holding it directly in the beam of the lantern light, which shines through the green glass and the dark liquid inside. I stare at it, trying to piece together where she's headed and find where we've gone wrong. Like the label, this theory must have a barely perceptible flaw.

"But the homemade stuff is never good," I say. "People bought wine from Vincent all over the place. And most people don't drink it. They just stash it in a cellar. But someone must open a bottle. Someone has to have tried it. If he's making it, wouldn't they notice that it's not right?"

"It could be like the art forger," she says. "The brush strokes. If Vincent's palate was as good as he said it was, he might have been able to recreate it from taste alone, until you couldn't tell his work from the original."

Or wine collectors are all snobs who want the prestige and never bother to check what's in the bottle. Both could also be true, I suppose.

"So Jean-Guy figured it out?" I ask. "That was why he came this weekend? To confront Vincent? But wouldn't it have gone the other way? If anyone was going to kill anyone in that confrontation, it would have been Vincent killing Jean-Guy." He wouldn't have nearly as good a story to print if Vincent were dead. Especially not if he were also busy dealing with a murder investigation where he would have been the prime suspect.

"It has to be someone else. Someone who found out and needed to cover it up. Someone who—"

Her hypothesis cuts off as the room plunges into darkness. The lantern. The propane must have finally burned out.

"Shit," she whispers.

"Where'd you go?" I ask. My fingers bump against some part of her arm, but eventually, I find her hand and hold tight.

"You okay?" she asks.

"Of course." I put my free hand out, fumbling along until I

collide with the base of the lantern. I follow it up, then hiss as the heat of the globe burns my fingertips.

"Want me to kiss it better?" she asks, and the idea of my fingers in her mouth makes me flush, but we have more important matters at hand, as it were.

"Focus," I say, jabbing a finger she can't see in her direction. "Someone killed Vincent and Jean-Guy, and you were about to piece together who it was and save us all."

She laughs in the dark, pulling me toward her. "I wouldn't go that far. I meant—"

Hurried footsteps come overhead, and Amanda cuts off whatever she was about to say. We freeze.

"Who's that?" I whisper.

"Shh." She pulls me away from the shelves, though I can't imagine she can see any better than I can. Yet she moves us quickly through the space, then tugs me down until I'm crouched against the wall. I put a hand out and find a solid panel in front of me. The door? Another shelf? I can't tell, and as I grope for more information, she takes hold of my wrist. Amanda presses my knuckles to her lips in a silent plea for stillness. I lean my head against her shoulder and close my eyes in the blackness of the cellar.

The footsteps are closer. Someone's coming down the stairs. Two people.

We hold our breaths and wait.

"It doesn't matter," a whispered voice says. "Let's get some rest."

"No. We have to do it now. Someone will start asking questions."

"What questions? What is going on?"

*Chris killed Vincent.* Didi had sounded so sure when she said that. I believed her. And now that the dust is settling, of course he would come to cover up his tracks . . . whatever those might be.

So imagine my surprise when it's not Chris and Laurel who come down the stairs. It's not even Sloan coming to protect her ever-diminishing earnings.

It's Bert and Didi, creeping down to the cellar and obviously trying very hard not to be noticed.

Something is very wrong.

# FIFTEEN

THE ROOM GLOWS DIMLY under the beam of a phone light. Turns out we're hiding behind one of the free-standing shelves opposite the door. I can't see Bert and Didi from here, and the room spins wildly as someone swings their phone from side to side like they're looking frantically for something.

"Here, Robert. The Domaine Saint-Arnault are all over here." Didi sounds annoyed. I've only heard her call him Robert a half dozen times in my whole life, and it's always when he's screwed up pretty seriously. Like the time he made a joke about how Sloan was looking more and more like a young lady and how she'd have to start wearing those short skirts to play tennis like all the other women at the club did. The edge of Didi's barked "Robert!" had heads turning from all directions.

Now, though, she sounds as weary as I do. Feet scuffle on the floor, and glass clinks together as bottles are moved around.

Bert curses softly. "No. No, this is wrong. These aren't all his. He didn't have that many. Some of them are Vincent's. How did they get down here?"

"What does it matter?"

"There's no need to use that tone," he says sullenly.

I glance at Amanda. Behind the shelf, it's so dark I can barely see her, but I'm pretty sure she's not looking at me, instead focusing all her energy on the conversation going on around us.

Bert sighs and mutters to himself. Bottles rattle.

"I need you to understand the gravity of the situation," he's saying. "If we can't figure out which of these were Vincent's and which are Arnold's, we're fucked. There will be no more cruises, Diane. No more galas."

"What are you talking about?"

There's more shuffling and bottles moving around, followed by a crash as something shatters.

"Now you've done it." Bert's voice is flat in a way I've never heard before. He can be short, but he's rarely angry. Now he sounds like he's a second away from actually hurting Didi, and the tone sends a chill down my spine.

"You've got lots more at home," she says. Bits of glass tinkle, like they're being pushed into a pile.

"No, I don't!" he shouts. "I don't. It's all shit at home, Didi."

"You didn't buy it to drink it, Robert. It's our nest egg. That's what you said."

"The egg is rotten." He's pulling bottles off the shelf. "Now help me grab these before anyone else comes down here. We'll take them all."

"Take them where? Bert, what's going on?"

Another crash, this time like a body being pushed against one of the shelves. Didi grunts, and I half rise up to help her before Amanda gets hold of my wrist and pulls me back down. It's still too dark to see her face, but she puts a finger to my lips, and the message is clear. Stay quiet. Stay hidden.

Didi is crying. Bert's still moving bottles.

"I don't understand," she says over a watery hiccup. "Why are you being like this?"

"Because we got screwed, all right?" he says. "Vincent screwed us. The wine is worthless. It's all fucking worthless."

My eyes go wide, even in the dark. The retirement fund he invested in wine. Bert's always bragging about it. But if Amanda's right and Vincent was somehow forging wines or selling them under the wrong label . . . Numbers tick over in my head. The wine in Dad's cellar could be worth tens or maybe even hundreds of thousands of dollars a bottle for the most expensive ones, but his collection isn't that big. Not compared to what Bert has, at least. Millions. If Dad's collection is in the thousands, then Bert's could be worth millions, and that doesn't include the money he's spent travelling to auctions and schmoozing other collectors.

My heart drops.

*Chris killed Vincent.* Didi either doesn't know or she's an excellent liar.

Based on the shock in her next question, I'm going with the first option. "What do you mean worthless?"

He growls. "That journalist. Jean-Guy. He didn't come here to write a profile. It was an exposé. He asked me tonight about wine forgery at the cocktail hour. Said he's been following Vincent's career and had proof that Vincent's been making his own wine for years and selling it off under other labels."

Didi gasps. "Isn't that illegal?"

"Of course it is. And we got sucked into it. Now take these bottles down to the dock."

The dock? What is his plan? Is he stealing Dad's wine? None of this makes any sense.

I'm not the only one with questions. Despite Bert's orders, Didi stands there, babbling words that barely form sentences. She's clearly trying to put the pieces together, and my heart goes out to her. If what Bert's saying is true, they've lost a lot of money. So much, and none of it is her fault. Though it's not

Bert's fault either. His anger is about more than fraud. They got duped. It happens. It's frustrating and expensive, but it doesn't explain why . . .

"Did you kill him?" Didi's question is soft and afraid, and Amanda and I are clinging so tightly to each other in the silence that follows that I'm going to have bruises on my arms later.

He doesn't answer. Just keeps stacking bottles. It sounds like he might be sliding them into the box Amanda brought down, and I still can't understand what his plan is. Not like you can swim cardboard across the lake, even if it's not weighed down by a dozen bottles of wine.

"Robert." She sounds on the verge of tears again. Her whole world is crumbling. "Did you kill him?"

He sighs, and when he speaks, it's like a child asking for forgiveness. "I didn't mean to. I just wanted to speak with him. But he wanted to show me one of his bottles of the '66, and after the conversation with Jean-Guy . . . I knew, Didi. Vinnie lied to us, and I was so mad. I was so angry. I'm sorry. I'm sorry." He's crying too now, sounding so lost. They were so happy when I arrived. The gracious hosts welcoming visitors into the fold. What must the rest of the night have been like for him, stuck with everyone and hoping no one asked questions he couldn't answer?

My fingertips are wet. My hands are over my mouth, and I realize tears are streaming down my cheeks too. What a mess.

There's a soft noise. Kissing. Nothing romantic. Just gentle comfort between people who have known each other for a long time.

"We'll figure it out," Didi says softly. "You weren't yourself. People will understand. Let's go find Gilly. She'll know what to do."

I freeze, and Amanda inhales beside me. The last time they saw me, we were on the dock. Will they assume we went to the boathouse? When they get there and realize I'm not there, what will they do? What will *I* do the next time I'm face-to-face with Bert? He killed someone. I'm sorry for all the money he lost, but that's not enough to justify killing someone. Two people, assuming Jean-Guy's death is his responsibility too. My father's best friend is a murderer.

The world tilts. Either Bert or Didi picks up the phone, making the shadows spin, and my head goes with it. I put a hand out to keep from falling on my face and collide with the shelf. The bottles inside rattle, and the sound of feet on the floor stops.

"Who's there?" Bert asks. The light is closer, and Amanda cranes her neck like she might be able to see over the top of the shelf. The footsteps come closer, and my heart beats so fast the dizziness comes back for a second. As it recedes, I make a decision, rising and pulling Amanda with me.

"It's us," I say, trying to make the statement sound whimsical. "Sorry, we were looking for—" My plan is to make it sound like we were looking for a quiet corner to make out, but I don't get that far. Bert and Didi are between us and the door. She's holding the phone, and when they see us, Bert grabs her, pulling her to him. I expect him to step in front of Didi like he's going to protect her, but instead, he wraps an arm around her throat and holds her against his chest like a human shield.

Then he pulls out a gun.

What the fuck? Where the fuck did he get a gun from?

"What did you hear?" he asks.

I shake my head. "Nothing. We were—"

"Bert?" Didi gasps, struggling against his massive forearm. When he doesn't let go, she lets out a yelp. "What are you doing?" She drops the phone, and it lands light-side up, bathing the space in a blue glow. The shadows are still oversize, but at least now I can see the gun Bert's holding isn't a handgun at all. It's the flare gun. The large barrel gapes at me, and even if I don't have to worry about bullets, a flare at this distance would still do more damage than I'm willing to chance.

"You'll make this worse if you hurt someone," Amanda says beside me. Yes. That's a better idea. Let her take charge.

"Shut up," he says, voice echoing off the walls. "It can't really get worse than it already is, can it?"

"Manslaughter," she says quietly in agreement. "With the lawyers you can afford, you'd probably get assault and probation. That's not so bad, is it?"

"Not so bad?" He laughs. "I'm going to lose everything. Do you know how much I spent at his auctions? Even if some of it was real, it doesn't matter. No one's going to buy it from me now."

"You still have the house," I say. "The cottage."

"Those aren't mine," he growls. "They're all in her name." He waves the flare gun toward Didi, and she whimpers. "She never let me have anything of my own. I had to work for every dollar I ever had."

I can't help myself when I sigh. Lord save us from entitled rich white masculinity. Doesn't have his name on the deed to their mansion or their luxury island property. Boo hoo. Whatever shall we do?

"Let her go," Amanda says again. "Let us all go. Let's go upstairs where we can talk about this—"

"And you can ask me to tell you how I did it? You already know."

"What about Jean-Guy?" I ask. I don't really care, but I have to keep him talking until Amanda can work out her next step.

He sneers. "Stuck-up little toad. Thought he was going to pull a gotcha moment on me. Even after Vincent was dead, he kept trying to pull me aside. Asked me questions. How much wine did I buy? How much research did I do on my own? He wanted me to say I didn't know any better. That Vincent had taken me for a fool. But that wasn't going to fix anything. If I admit how much I trusted him, how does that make me look? I'd never be able to see any of my friends again. Never be able to travel."

The monologue is still so very "poor me," and I have no sympathy.

"So you killed him? So you could still jet off to Paris in the spring?"

"But you were in bed," Didi says, still trying to save things as her world falls apart around her. "We went to bed together."

"You'd sleep through an earthquake with that meditation app of yours. I couldn't settle, so I went outside to clear my head and Jean-Guy was there. I pushed him because he was trying to spoil my weekend with his accusations." He spits the words. "He died because the railing gave way. That's not my fault."

"Then you should have spoken up."

"I've lost everything." He sounds genuinely pained, and I can't believe his perspective is so skewed. "It's not fair."

"Not fair?" From the hall, voices start coming. We've been shouting and no doubt woken the kitchen staff sleeping in the rec room. "Not fair? That's bullshit, Bert. Guess what's not fair? My dad having a heart attack in the middle of the night out here all by himself. Not fair is not getting to say goodbye. Not fair is a sister who thinks everything can be solved if we sell all his shit. That's not fair. What you're going through is—" But I don't get to finish. As I yell, Amanda springs forward, launching herself at Bert and Didi. At the last second, I remember her saying hand-to-hand combat isn't part of her spy skillset. She's fast, but he's big, and they crash to the ground together. Didi cries out at the impact, and someone kicks the phone away. It skitters over the floor, then goes dark, leaving the whole room in black, with nothing but the sound of a fight to help orient me.

"Amanda?" I ask, but there's no reply. She grunts, and he curses. Didi screams.

"What's going on?" someone calls from down the hall. Someone else runs into me. Or rolls, maybe. I crash down to the floor, bouncing my head off something hard as I go. Bright stars shoot up in my vision, then there's a crack and a sizzle as the whole room goes red.

The flare gun.

# SIXTEEN

IN THE MOMENT OF ILLUMINATION, Amanda and Bert are on the floor, both of them with a grasp on the gun. In the contained space of the cellar, the light is so bright I have to close my eyes against it. But when I open them again, the light consumes the white shape of the cardboard box Bert was stuffing with bottles.

"No!" Bert says, releasing the gun and rushing toward the burning box. He reaches for it as Didi shouts in warning, then hisses—because what else are you going to do when you stick your hand in a fire?—and pulls the whole shelf over instead in a giant heave. Unfortunately, along with the crash of wine, the stack of paper that was Vincent's auction program also tumbles to the ground in a fluttering downpour of white that almost immediately starts to crinkle and burn as it piles on top of the burning box.

"We have to go," Amanda says.

"The wine!" Bert flails like he's still looking for a way to stop what's happened. But the wooden shelves and the box of paper inventory sheets make it nearly impossible.

It's Didi who brings him to his senses, literally slapping him across the face with a force that makes me wince.

"Forget about your goddamn wine, Robert. Grow up, and get us out of here."

I wish I could say he leaps into action to save us, but he still hesitates, gaze bouncing between the door and the first shelf that is quickly going black as the flames lick up its side. Finally, Didi grabs hold of him and drags him to the door.

"I'm sorry," he says quietly. "I didn't know the gun would go off."

I'm really not in the mood for his apologies.

The kitchen staff are in the hall looking confused, but the smoke already billowing from the cellar door is enough to send them up the stairs. They don't ask any questions, and I'm not sure what I'd tell them anyway.

"We have to get the others," I say, pushing through the kitchen toward the guest wing.

"Gillian, wait!" Amanda calls, but I don't stop.

There aren't many others to get at this point, which is a small mercy. Chris and Laurel are in the first room. I don't have time to ask questions about what happened to sleeping alone. I shake them awake and tell them to go to the water, which they do, though Chris keeps saying something about "so many more followers after this" as he leaves.

Sloan is more complicated. She's in the room at the end of the hall. And she's drunk. Or worse. There are two empty wine bottles on the floor, and there's a pool of acrid purple around her where she's fallen asleep on the old quilt with a third bottle beside her.

Huh. The sun must be finally rising if I can make all that out with no light. It's been a long time since I saw daylight.

"Sloan. Sloan!" I shake her. She doesn't respond, not even to squeeze her eyes tighter and tell me to get lost. "For god's sake, Sloan, wake up."

I'm about to check to see if she even has a pulse when Amanda appears in the doorway.

"We have to leave," she says. "The fire's coming up the stairs."

"Help me," I say, tugging at Sloan's arm. Unconscious, my sister might as well weigh a million tonnes.

"I got her." Amanda strides across the room and pulls Sloan up and over onto her shoulder, carrying her out like a firefighter. If only we had a real one of those now.

"Bruno? Is it time to go?" Sloan slurs as we rush for an exit. The hall is hazy with smoke, and I cough as we run through the kitchen. Outside, the teetering deck seems like the lesser of two evils, and neither of us takes much care picking our way down the ruined steps. The heat behind us is building, and we need to get to safety.

On the dock, the scene is predictably chaotic. The kitchen staff are all in life jackets like our emergency water landing is imminent, and it probably is. Bert is sitting by the boathouse with his head in his hands while Didi lectures him. Chris is trying to pick a fight with both of them, and Laurel is wrapped around his back like a monkey, trying to slow him down.

"I knew it was you!" he says, unperturbed by his girlfriend's protests. "You're a killer." He fishes his phone from his pocket and holds it toward Bert while Didi puts up a hand, trying to block his camera. "You're lucky I can't livestream this right now, but as soon as I have a signal, I'm telling everyone what you've done. You can't stop me. I can film you without your permission." The last part comes in a crow of triumph that has me rolling my eyes.

Chris takes a step back, no doubt trying to frame his shot for maximum effect. But as he does, his heel slips on the edge of the dock, and he overbalances. Behind him, Laurel shrieks as he tips backward, but it's too late for both of them. Chris's phone goes flying as he wheels his arms, but gravity has already won this fight, and they both topple backward into the lake with a splash.

Amanda is setting Sloan down. She's still not coherent, but she keeps muttering to an imaginary Bruno, so at least she's alive. I couldn't handle one more dead body in a twenty-four-hour period. Even Sloan's.

Behind us, the house is burning. Flames are already licking out the basement windows, and orange light flickers from the top too. With the rising light, the scale of the damage from the storm is tremendous. The tree that went through the roof must be over a hundred feet tall, dwarfing the house. And that's not even considering what's about to happen with the fire.

As if to prove the point, there's a popping sound, and we all take an involuntary step back as the tree catches fire. The pine pitch goes up like a bomb, taking the rest of the structure with it.

"Look." One of the kitchen staff—oh, it's Kennedy—points toward the water, and we all turn in the direction she indicates. The sun is on the horizon, casting orange and purple ripples on the lake. Two boats are headed toward us, their noses thrusting upward as they hurry through the early morning calm.

Rescue. If there's anything left to rescue. The house is well and truly ablaze now. Nothing to save. Even some of the trees around it are starting to light up. By the time the boats arrive and more help is called, there will be nothing left but the island itself.

———

And there isn't. The first boats to arrive are neighbours, alerted by the smoke on the sunrise. They've brought the communal fire pumps that many of the houses have out here, but by the time they're set up and we have enough people to use them, the only thing left to save is the boathouse, and even that is questionable. Turns out it's also leaning pretty heavily; we just couldn't see it in the dark. A police boat arrives shortly after. They take Bert and Didi and hurry away. Chris tries to insist he needs to come too as a witness, but no one believes he has anything valuable to contribute. Not even Laurel, finally. Her unexpected dunking was the last straw, and she sits apart from him, glaring from behind her wet hair.

Murray has also come along, bringing blankets and hot coffee for the rest of us, and we huddle on his boat watching so many of my memories go down in flames.

"The insurance on this is going to be a bitch," I say as I sip my thermos, then grimace when I remember there is no insurance. Just a rock with a ruined house. Amanda and I are sitting together on the bow. Sloan is close by, puking bright purple into the lake to pay for all the wine she downed. She's lucky she didn't give herself alcohol poisoning, though the way her complexion keeps changing from paper white to putty grey says she might disagree with me on that point. She says, "I'm not dealing with that. That's your job."

Typical.

"I thought you were going to sell it?" I ask sweetly.

She swings a wobbly arm in the direction of the smouldering island. "Who would want it now?"

Who indeed? Honestly, I'm not sure what I'll be able to do with it either, but at least we have time to decide.

There are more police cars waiting for us at the marina. Also a man in a grey suit. He stands by a black town car, talking in hushed but hurried words on his cell phone.

"Your ride?" I ask.

Amanda watches him, mouth pressed together in a grim line, but eventually she nods.

"Will he take you to the police station?" I ask.

"Probably not."

There's a black smudge on her cheek, and when I go to rub it away, she takes my hand and lifts it up higher, like she might kiss the knuckles. I pull away before she can.

"Don't," I say.

She tilts her head sadly. "Gil."

But it's too much. After everything, these are feelings I can't feel right now. Not when the underlying truth is the same. Last time, our breakup felt endless. Today, I'll make sure it's fast. Tear off the old Band-Aid and wait for things to heal on their own.

They're loading Sloan into an ambulance, and I back slowly away from Amanda toward it.

"It was nice to see you again," I say with what I hope is a charming smile. "Take care of yourself. Say hi to the art forger if you're ever in Montreal again."

She looks like she's going to argue, but the man in the suit is walking toward her, and the expression on his face says he won't tolerate any dockside profession of love.

Neither will I. I walked away from her once, and I can do it again.

The black car is already pulling out of the parking lot before they get the ambulance doors closed.

# SEVENTEEN



SIX MONTHS *later*

"And the winner of the Arnold Fletcher Prize for Best First Canadian Novel is . . ." The woman in the evening gown beams at the audience. Around me, people lean forward in anticipation. She flicks open the envelope and pulls the card free, and her smile grows wide before she says, "*Linking Gerrard* by Aarav Khurana!"

The assembled crowd cheers. Forks are clinked against wine glasses. Diamond rings flash in the banquet hall lights. Aarav, looking a little starstruck, stands from his table close to the stage and makes his way through the congratulatory onlookers. He shakes hands with some of the other nominees who are no doubt doing their best to appear gracious in case the cameras are watching while quickly spiraling into vortexes of self-loathing while they wonder what they did wrong that Aarav won and they didn't.

It's a good book. Dad would have liked it. The story of a young man trying to balance his life in Toronto with the expectations of his traditional Indian family who has moved from Mumbai to live with him. It's smart and funny, and while I've never had an Indian grandmother begging me to give up my debauched Western lifestyle and get married, the themes of family conflict and the competing desires for independence and belonging are all too familiar.

Speaking of which, the two empty seats beside me are a mixed blessing. I'm glad I didn't have to listen to Sloan and Bruno bitch for two hours about how their three season room leaks in the winter. She called me in tears earlier because apparently one of Bruno's canvases was destroyed when the warm wave of not-quite-spring temperatures melted the snow on Tabitha and Luigi's creation and the water had the audacity to find its way in instead of staying outside.

"He didn't even get a chance to start the painting!" Sloan wailed on the phone, which made the tragedy all the more confusing. Is she telling me her night is ruined because of a trickle of water on a blank canvas? He could probably let it dry and sell it for a fortune.

Still, their absence means I've avoided the pleasure of their company, but it also means I've been forced to repeat myself a dozen times to the doddering nonagenarian sitting next to me during dinner. I think she might have been married to a former governor general. Or she worked for the governor general? Her name is Doreen, and her stories are rambling at best. I'd already given up keeping track of them before our salad plates had been taken away.

Doreen pats my hand and gives me a wobbling smile. "You'll get them next time, dear."

I smile back. I've already explained three times that Arnold was my dad and that I'm representing his family. She somehow got that confused and has decided I was one of the nominees for the award.

She flags down a waiter, no doubt to ask for a third scotch on the rocks, which she's been putting away neatly all evening.

Since the award's been awarded and there's nothing left to do but applaud Aarav one more time when he's done his speech, then applaud one another for having the good literary taste to be part of this event, I might as well follow Doreen's lead.

I reach for the bottle of red wine at the centre of the table. Chateau des Charmes, Niagara VQA. I can buy the same bottle for fifteen bucks at the liquor store on my way home. Tastes nice, though. Black cherry and licorice.

"I'll have a glass if you're pouring."

The voice next to me is smooth and smoky like fine wine. Finer wine than what you serve to two hundred people at a literary prize gala. The sound makes me freeze in place, sloshing wine over the lip of my glass and onto the white tablecloth. Amanda has to tip it upward again before I pour the whole thing all over the centrepiece.

I blink rapidly, like if I do it enough, I'll wake from this dream. The one where she's slipped into the seat next to mine and is watching me with a velvety smile. Her hair is pulled back against her scalp, and she's wearing a navy and white cocktail dress with a white cardigan held in place by a gold chain draped over her shoulders. She looks like an upscale sexy librarian.

My throat is so dry I can barely swallow. She takes the bottle from me and pours some into the empty wine glass in front of Sloan's unused place setting. My hand shakes as I lift my own glass to my lips and take a sip . . . then take a longer one as I try to settle my jangling nerves and racing heartbeat.

She watches me with an amused arch of her eyebrow.

"Hey, Gil," she says.

"What are you doing here?" I ask, then slump as I realize. She's working. Two hundred people in this ballroom. Wealthy and well-connected. It's what she does.

"I was hoping to see you," she says.

I snort on my next sip of wine and have to use a napkin before it dribbles down my chin.

"In between chasing down money launderers? Don't think there's much chance of making it big here when most people can buy the same book at Indigo tomorrow morning."

Her lips press tight. She's wearing a soft pink lip gloss, and I can practically taste it just looking at her. I finish my glass of wine and reach to pour another, but she intercepts me, taking my hand and shaking it like we've just met.

"Hi," she says, holding my gaze. "My name is Amanda Mulgrave. I work in wealth management. What do you do?"

I scoff, but she grips my hand tight, and there's something in her expression I haven't seen before. It's hesitant. Tentative.

"Gillian Fletcher," I say slowly. "I'm a graphic designer."

She nods like this is all new information. "And what's your connection to the event tonight?"

I roll my eyes, but she's still holding my hand, so I say, "Arnold Fletcher was my father."

Her mouth drops open. "No way! For real? *Frost Burn* is one of my favourite books."

Now I can't hold back my laughter. "I think you're pushing your cover story too hard here. *Frost Burn* is no one's favourite book unless you're a pretentious literary dickhead. Everyone hates being forced to read it in high school, and no one ever gets over that resentment."

Amanda's shiny pink lips are quivering at the corners as she tries to swallow her own laughter. "Fair enough. But I really am a wealth manager."

I pull my hand free. This is getting awkward.

Beside me, Doreen suddenly asks, "What did she say?" and I remember we're not alone. In fact, I'm very relieved for her interruption.

I lean in so I can basically shout directly into her ear.

"This is Amanda Mulgrave. She's a wealth manager."

"A what?" Doreen frowns. "A shelf brander?"

I stand, pushing my chair in and resting a hand on each of their shoulders. "I'll leave you to get better acquainted."

Sometimes the bravest and best strategy is retreat.

I didn't count on being hung up at the coat check, though.

"Are you sure you have the right tag?" the girl at the counter asks.

"Pretty sure," I say. There's a line forming behind me, and a dozen sets of eyes are practically boring into the back of my neck, because the mystery of the missing black wool coat is clearly my fault. Never mind that easily half the women here tonight probably wore something nearly identical. It's the uniform of women over thirty in downtown Toronto from November to April.

The coat check girl gives me a game smile. "Then we'll find it. Don't you worry."

"It's that one there." Amanda is standing next to me, once again appearing out of nowhere. I jump. But sure enough, she's pointing to the first coat on the rack next to the one the girl is desperately pawing through, and there's my coat. Dad's old caramel and cream houndstooth scarf dangles from the sleeve where I stuffed it on my way in.

Coat returned, I don't wait for Amanda to retrieve hers. I throw mine on and make a break for the elevator. Hopefully, she takes the hint. I haven't heard from Amanda since the house burned down. The last six months have been a mess of conversations with police—Bert pleaded guilty before he'd even been formally charged, did four months at a correctional facility, and is now serving a commuted manslaughter sentence at the house on Channel Island due to prison overcrowding—and dead end phone calls with insurance providers who can't help, contractors who catch a glimpse of the charred remains of Dad's house and basically run away screaming, and journalists who want to write a story about what *really* happened that night but only call back once or twice before they realize I really don't care to tell them. At no time have I heard from or thought of Amanda Mulgrave.

That last part's not true. I thought of her. A lot. At least at first. I thought about calling her. Just showing up at her office. I mooned over her photo on the firm's website more than a woman with any self-respect should for a few weeks, but a month later the picture and her bio disappeared, and I took that as a sign. Whatever the fallout was from Ross Island, she'd been moved. Her cover was blown, and her task force or whoever needed to relocate her somewhere.

And yet, as the elevator doors open, here she is. She's breathing hard, and a few strands of hair have escaped from her tight bun.

"Did you run down the stairs to beat the elevator?" I ask.

"I need to speak to you," she says.

"I can't," I say.

"Please."

"No. Not as long as you're a . . . ." I glance at the couple standing behind her, clearly waiting to get on the elevator. "A wealth manager." Hopefully, the arch of my eyebrows means the *you're a spy* subtext is clear.

The elevator doors start to close between us. At the last second, she leaps forward, squeezing between them. I have to step back to avoid being knocked over. The couple protests as Amanda stabs at the button to make sure the doors slide all the way shut.

"Sorry," she says. "Take the next one."

"What are you doing?" I ask as she pushes the button to take us to the top floor.

"One drink," she says. "Please. Have one drink with me. That's all."

I wrinkle my nose and make a strangled groaning sound. This is a terrible idea on so many fronts. I'm slowly overheating in my coat, and Amanda is too close for comfort, and this hotel has the slowest elevators known to humanity, which makes the journey upward painful.

But finally, the doors open, and we're looking into the dim space of the penthouse bar. It's enclosed, and Toronto sparkles outside, office buildings and the CN Tower glittering against the late winter sky.

When she puts her hand in mine, I melt.

"Fine," I say, tugging the scarf from my neck. "One drink. And it's going to be a small one."

The bar is mostly empty. It's a Wednesday night in February. Not exactly peak Toronto tourist season. We take seats in a dark corner away from any of the other patrons. Amanda orders a glass of cab franc. I order a shot of Jameson. She watches me with an amused grin as the server sets both down in front of us.

"Told you it would be small," I say, lifting my shot glass toward her in a toast. The effect is weakened as I tilt the glass to my lips and cough at the alcohol fumes hitting the back of my throat on an inhale. Whiskey slips over my fingers, and half the glass is empty before I manage to get it back on the table. I try to muffle the cough in my sleeve, but it's a bad one. My eyes water, and my ears burn.

Amanda is smugly sipping her cab franc, waiting for me to recover. I dab at my eyes with a paper napkin that comes back with black smears on it. Dammit. Now my mascara is running.

"You okay?" she asks.

"Fine," I wheeze. I pour the last of the whiskey down my throat, though it's unsatisfying after everything. "Fine. This has been fun. Gotta go."

"I quit my job," she says hurriedly as I stand.

"Good for you." The scarf has fallen on the floor, and I bend to retrieve it.

"No," she says. "I *quit* my *job*."

The way she emphasizes the words makes me pause. I wrap the scarf up in my fist and sit back down.

"Your job?" I ask. "Or your *job*?"

She glances around. No one is close enough to hear.

"Both," she says.

"Why?" The back of my throat tingles and the whiskey burns hot in my gut, but there's something that burns brighter next to it. Hope. Silly, pathetic hope that this is it. That finally, things will be different.

She shrugs. "Too many secrets. It was getting tiring. Hard to spend time with the people I care about when I can't tell them the truth."

The hope flares bright, consuming the alcohol. My nerve endings zing like fireflies. This is it. This is it.

"So what will you do now?" I picture her lounging in her apartment, dressed in silk pyjamas while soft music plays. I picture myself next to her, head against her chest, knee between her thighs.

"I got a job in London," she says.

"London, Ontario?" I ask.

"No." Amanda grins a lopsided grin. "London, England."

"Oh." The hope snuffs out, and I'm left with the sour taste of alcohol I will regret tomorrow.

"A guy I know runs a hedge fund there. He needs a partner."

I'm the one who needs a partner. The thought hits me between the eyes so hard a tear slips out, and I wipe it away on the mascara-stained napkin.

"So you really are a wealth manager," I say.

"Plain and simple."

Plain and simple. Just like the pain is simple. It's the pain of being left behind. Again. I didn't think I'd see her again, and now that she's here, she's leaving. What even was the point of her showing up?

"I thought you might come with me," she says.

"To London?"

"Yeah."

"Why?" I can't even fathom what's going on here. Is she looking for a cover? Two lesbians setting up shop in a foreign country? Someone to divert attention at new parties and functions while she chats up art forgers and assassins?

"Because I love you," she says. "I want to be in your life and make you happy."

I should tell her that's not how to do it. Showing up six months later and asking me to drop everything to move across the ocean isn't her being in my life. It's me being in hers, yet again.

But even as I work up the protests, they die in my whiskey-tinged throat. What really is my life? Sloan and I don't talk unless we have to. Bert and Didi are basically recluses these days, too embarrassed to show their faces. The friends I have are still more colleagues and acquaintances than real friends. Even my job doesn't tie me here. I started working for a new advertising agency right before Thanksgiving. All the work is remote, and the people I speak with most are the project manager in California and a digital nomad freelancer in Malaysia. We leave emails and Slack messages like breadcrumbs for each other to find when we wake up and log in. What would it matter if I'm sending them from Toronto or London?

"I'd have to sell my condo," I say, but even I can hear this is an acquiescence, not a protest. Amanda's smile is radiant.

"I have a contact," she says. "We could get it listed this week."

"Of course you have a contact." This is how she is. Spy or no spy, she has ways. Networks. The truth is sitting before me as plain as day.

"Please." She wraps her hands around mine on the table, and the gesture feels so perfect. Comforting. "I have a flat in Hampstead. It has a view of the heath. You'll love it."

I probably would. I've never been to London. Double-decker busses. The royal family. That's all I've got.

And Amanda.

Is that enough?

She must see me hesitate because she scoots her chair around the table so we're seated next to each other.

"No more lies," she says. "I promise to tell you everything. I have nothing to hide."

"Because you're only a wealth manager now?" I ask slowly.

"Yes." She says it breathlessly, but there's a flicker behind her gaze that says there's more to the story. Did she really give it up for me? Are we about to become some international crime-fighting duo?

Does it matter?

Once upon a time I made a deal with a wicked witch. The witch was Sloan, and we agreed not to do anything major with our lives for a year after Dad died. Clearly, that worked out well. But it'll be a year next week since the heart attack. Surely that's close enough.

Once upon a time I met a princess, and even in the years we weren't together, she's the only one I wanted. We've survived murder ballerinas, wine forgers, and house fires, after all. And that was one night. Surely we can survive life in a Hampstead flat while mixing and mingling with the who's who of London finance. Who knows? I might meet a hitman pretending to be a supermodel or the greatest art forger in the world who works as a gallery curator by day. It'll make a good story, and Amanda will be there to help me make sense of it.

"Your place is closer than mine," I say, untangling our hands so I can pull her to her feet. If we're going to spend our life together, no sense in not starting now.

She smiles. "Closer than you think."

"What do you mean?"

Amanda stubs a finger on the table, pointing downward. "Fifteenth floor."

"Of the hotel?"

She arches an eyebrow. "I gave up the condo last month when the job offer came through. I'm flying out tomorrow, but I had to see you once before—"

Guess what? It doesn't matter. She has lots of time to tell me the truth. All of it. Right now, I have other things on my mind. I lunge forward, framing her face with my palms, and kiss her. She squeaks, stopping midsentence, but very quickly catches up with the shift in gears.

Kissing her has always been easy, especially now that it's not filled with half-truths and regret or the scent of wine and blood lingering in the air. We're both gasping by the time I break away. The bartender is doing his very best not to look at us when he very clearly wants to continue to watch the lesbians kissing more than anything. Amanda flicks an eyebrow at me and pulls me in one more time, just for our own amusement.

"Fifteenth floor?" I say when I can breathe again.

"Mm-hmm."

"And you're leaving tomorrow?"

"Was going to. I can put it off for a few days if you want."

"Let's see how tonight goes." I pick the scarf off the floor once more and head for the elevators. I already know how tonight is going to go. It's going to be amazing.

As long as we're under the same roof, everything will be all right.

# ABOUT THE AUTHOR

Allison lives in Toronto with her very patient husband and the world's cutest team of rescue pets. She tries to split her time between writing, exploring Toronto's parks, and traveling anywhere that has good wine. Tragically, this leaves no time to clean the house.

# LGBTQ+ ROMANCES BY ALLISON TEMPLE

### Out & About

Work-Love Balance

Honeymoon Sweet

### The Seacroft Series

Top Shelf

Cold Pressed

Hot Potato

### Shared Series

My Not-So-Super Blind Date (part of Subparheroes)

Under Her Roof (part of Accidentally Undercover)

Puppuccino (part of Bold Brew)

### Standalone

Destination Bedding

The Neighbourly Thing

Up North

Boyfriend With Benefits

The Pick Up

LGBTQ+ FANTASY BY ALLI TEMPLE

**Afterlife Incorporated**

Only Mostly Dead

Hate to Haunt You (coming soon)

**The Pirate & Her Princess**

Uncharted

Unbroken

Unleashed

www.ingramcontent.com/pod-product-compliance
Lightning Source LLC
Chambersburg PA
CBHW071418300726
48976CB00004B/1165